UNDERGROUND TIME

UNDERGROUND TIME

A Novel

Delphine de Vigan

*Translated from the French
by George Miller*

BLOOMSBURY

NEW YORK · BERLIN · LONDON · SYDNEY

Liberté • Égalité • Fraternité
RÉPUBLIQUE FRANÇAISE

This book is supported by the French Ministry of Foreign Affairs,
as part of the Burgess program run by the Cultural Department of the
French Embassy in London (www.frenchbooknews.com)

Published by Bloomsbury USA, New York

All papers used by Bloomsbury USA are natural, recyclable products
made from wood grown in well-managed forests. The manufacturing
processes conform to the environmental regulations of the country of origin.

Vigan, Delphine de.
[Heures souterraines. English]
Underground time / Delphine de Vigan ; translated from the French by George Miller.
— 1st U.S. ed.
p. cm.
ISBN-13: 978-1-60819-712-5 (pbk.)
ISBN-10: 1-60819-712-3 (pbk.)
I. Miller, George, 1965–
II. Title.
PQ2722.I43H4813 2011
843'.92—dc22
2011015031

First published in France by J.C. Lattès as *Les heures souterraines* in 2009
First published in the United States by Bloomsbury USA in 2011

1 3 5 7 9 10 8 6 4 2

Typeset by Hewer Text UK Ltd, Edinburgh
Printed in the U.S.A. by Quad/Graphics, Fairfield, Pennsylvania

To Alfia Delanoe

On voit de toutes petites choses qui luisent
Ce sont des gens dans des chemises
Comme durant ces siècles de la longue nuit
Dans le silence et dans le bruit.

Comme un Lego, Gérard Manset

The voice cuts through her sleep and hovers on the surface. The woman is stroking some playing cards which are face down on the table. She repeats several times with conviction: 'On the twentieth of May your life will change.'

Mathilde doesn't know if she's still dreaming or has already begun the new day. She glances at the radio-alarm. It's four in the morning.

She *was* dreaming. The dream was about the woman she saw a few weeks ago. She was a clairvoyant – there, she's admitted it – she didn't have a shawl or crystal ball, but she was a clairvoyant none the less. Mathilde took the metro all the way across Paris, sat behind the thick curtains of a ground-floor flat in the sixteenth arrondissement and handed over €150 to have her palm and her numbers read. She went there because she had nothing else left: no glimmer of light to reach towards, no future tense, no prospect of anything after. She went because you need something to hang on to.

Afterwards she went off with her handbag swinging from her hand and that ridiculous prediction, as if it were written in the lines of her palm, her date of birth or the eight letters of her first name, as if it were visible to the naked eye: a man on 20 May. A man who would save her at this turning point in her life. It just goes to show, you can hold a masters in econometrics and applied statistics and still consult a clairvoyant. A few days later it dawned on her that she'd thrown €150 down the drain, it was as simple as that. That's what she was thinking as she went through her monthly bank statement with a red pen, and that she didn't give a damn about 20 May or any other day for that matter.

But 20 May remained a sort of vague promise hanging over the abyss.

Today's the day.

Today something could happen, something important. An event that would change the course of her life, mark a point of departure, a break with the past. For several weeks it's been there in her diary in black ink. An Event with a capital E, which she's been waiting for like a rescue on the high seas.

Today, 20 May, because she has reached the end, the end of what she can bear, the end of what it's humanly possible to bear. It's written in the book of life. In the shifting sky, in the conjunction of the planets, in the shimmer of numbers. It's written that today she will have reached this exact point, the point of no return, where nothing ordinary can change the passage of the hours, where nothing can happen without threatening her whole universe, without calling everything into question. Something has got to happen. Something completely exceptional. To get her out of this. To make it stop.

In the past few weeks she's imagined everything: the possible and the impossible, the best and the worst. That she would be the victim of an attack, that in the middle of the long corridor between the metro and the RER a powerful bomb would go off, that it would blow everything up. Her body would be annihilated, she would be scattered in the stifling air of the morning rush hour, blown to the four corners of the station. Later they'd find pieces of her floral print dress and her travelcard. Or she'd break her ankle. She'd slip stupidly on one of those greasy patches you sometimes have to walk around that look shiny on the light tiles, or else she'd miss the first step of the escalator and fall awkwardly. They'd have to call the fire brigade, operate on her, screw in plates and pins. She'd be unable to move for months. Or she'd be kidnapped by mistake in broad daylight by some obscure splinter group. Or she'd meet a man on the train or in the station café, a man who'd say to her, 'Madam, you can't go on like this. Give me your hand. Take my arm. Let's go back. Put your bag down. Don't stay standing there. Sit down here. It's over. You're not going to go back there any more. You can't. You're going to fight. *We're* going to fight. I'll be by your side.' A man or a woman, in fact – it didn't matter. Someone who'd understand that she couldn't go on any more, that with every passing day she was eating into her very substance, into her essence. Someone who'd stroke her cheek or hair, who'd murmur as though to himself, 'How have you managed to keep going so long? How did you find the courage, the strength?' Someone who'd rebel. Who'd say, 'Enough.' Who would take charge of her. Someone who would make her get off one stop early or who'd sit down opposite her at the back of a bar. Who would watch the hours go by on the wall clock. At noon, he or she would smile at her and say: 'There, it's over.'

It's night. The night before the day that she's been waiting for against her better judgement. It's four in the morning. Mathilde knows she won't get back to sleep, she knows the scenario off by heart, the positions she'll try one by one, the effort she'll make to calm her breathing, the pillow she'll wedge under her neck. And then she'll end up turning on the light, picking up a

4

book she won't manage to get into. She'll look at her children's drawings pinned to the wall, so as not to think, not to anticipate the day ahead.

Not see herself getting off the train,
Not see herself saying good morning while wanting
    to scream,
Not see herself walking soundlessly across the grey
    carpet,
Not see herself sitting at that desk.

She stretches her limbs one by one. She feels hot. The dream is still there. The woman is holding her upturned palm. She repeats one last time: 20 May.

Mathilde hasn't been able to sleep for ages. Nearly every night at the same time anxiety wakes her. She knows the order in which she will have to cope with the images, the doubts, the questions. She knows by heart the twists and turns of insomnia. She knows she'll have to run through everything from the start: how it began, how it got worse, how she got here, and how she cannot go back. Already her heart is beating more quickly. The machine that crushes everything is up and running, and everything goes through it: the shopping she has to do, the appointments she needs to make, the friends she must call, the bills she mustn't forget, somewhere to rent for the summer . . . All the things that used to be so easy which have now become so hard.

Lying in the sweaty sheets, she always comes to the same conclusion: she's not going to make it.

S urely he isn't going to cry like an idiot, sitting on the toilet seat in a hotel bathroom at four in the morning?

He's wearing the dressing gown that Lila put on when she got out of the shower. He smells the fabric, seeking the perfume he loves so much. He looks at himself in the mirror. He's almost as pale as the sink. On the floor his feet search out the softness of the rug. Lila's asleep in the bedroom, her arms folded. She fell asleep after they made love, straight away. She began snoring softly. She always snores when she's been drinking.

As she fell asleep she murmured 'thank you'. That's what did for him. It went right through him. She said thank you.

She says thank you for everything. Thank you for the meal, for the night, for the weekend, for making love, for calling. Thank you when he asks how she is.

She grants him her body, some of her time, and her rather remote presence. She knows that he gives, and she doesn't reveal anything of herself, nothing that really matters.

He got up carefully so as not to wake her and felt his way to the bathroom in the dark. When he got there, he stretched out his hand to turn on the light and closed the door.

A little while earlier, when they got back from dinner, as she was undressing, she asked, 'What is it you need?'

What do you need, what do you lack, what would you like, what do you dream of? Through some sort of blindness that may be temporary or permanent she often asks him these questions. This type of question. With all the candour of a twenty-eight-year-old. This evening he almost answered: 'I need to grip the balcony rail and scream until I'm out of breath. Do you think that would be possible?'

But he didn't.

They've spent the weekend in Honfleur. They walked along the beach, wandered around town. He bought her a dress and some flip-flops. They had some wine, ate in a restaurant, stayed in bed with the curtains drawn amid the mingled smells of perfume and sex. They'll leave tomorrow morning first thing and he'll drop her off outside her building. Rose's voice will tell him where his first appointment is. His Renault Clio will take him to his first patient, then to a second. He'll drown as he does every day in a tide of symptoms and loneliness, sink into the sticky grey city.

They've had other weekends like this one.

They're interludes which she grants him – far from Paris and from everything else – less and less often.

You'd only have to look at them when she walks beside him, never brushing against him or touching him. You'd only have to see them in a restaurant or on any café terrace, and that distance which separates them. You'd only have to look down at them, by some swimming pool, their bodies side by side, the caresses she doesn't return and which he has given up on. It would be enough to see them anywhere, in Toulouse, Barcelona or Paris, in any city at all, him stumbling on the paving stones and tripping over the kerb, unbalanced, caught out.

At times like these she says: 'God, you're clumsy!'

Then he'd like to say no. He'd like to say: 'Before I met you I was an eagle, I was a bird of prey. Before I met you I flew above the streets and didn't bump into anything. Before I met you I was strong.'

It's four in the morning and he's acting like a complete idiot, shut in a hotel bathroom because he can't sleep.

He can't sleep because he loves her and she doesn't give a damn.

Though she offers herself to him in darkened bedrooms.

Though he can take her, caress and lick her, he can penetrate her standing up, sitting down, on his knees. Though she gives him her mouth, her breasts, her buttocks, imposes no limit on him, though she gulps down his sperm.

But away from the bed, Lila escapes him. She slips away. Away from the bed, she doesn't kiss him, doesn't slip her hand round his back or stroke his cheek. She scarcely looks at him.

Away from the bed, he has no body, or else has a body whose substance she doesn't notice. She's unaware of his skin.

One by one he sniffs the bottles on the sink: moisturiser, shampoo, shower gel in their wicker basket. He splashes some water on his face, dries it with a towel folded on the radiator. He goes through the times he's spent with her since they met, remembering everything from the day that Lila took his hand as they left a café one winter evening when he couldn't face going home.

Even at the beginning he didn't try to resist, he allowed himself to slide. He remembers everything, and everything agrees; it all points in the same direction. If he thinks about it, Lila's behaviour shows her lack of enthusiasm better than all her words, her way of being there without being there, her walk-on part, except for once or twice perhaps when he thought for a night that something more than the obscure need she had for him was possible.

Wasn't that what she said to him, that night or some other? 'I need you. Can you understand that, Thibault, without thinking it's about subservience or dependence?'

She had taken hold of his arm and repeated: 'I need you.'

Now she thanks him for being there. While she waits for something better.

She's not afraid of losing him, of deceiving him, of displeasing him. She's not afraid of anything. She couldn't care less.

And there's nothing he can do about that.

He has to leave her. It has to stop.

He's old enough to know that what's done is done. Lila just isn't programmed to fall in love with him. These things are written inside people like data in a computer. Lila doesn't *recognise* him in the computing sense of the term, just as some computers can't read a document or open certain disks. It's not in her specifications, her set-up.

Whatever he does, whatever he says, whatever he tries to input.

He is too sensitive, too easily hurt, too involved, too emotional. Not distant enough, not chic enough, not mysterious enough.

He's not enough.

The die is cast. He's lived long enough to know that he has to move on, draw a line, get out.

He'll tell her in the morning, when the alarm call wakes them.

Monday the twentieth of May strikes him as a good date, it's got the right ring to it.

But tonight, like every night for more than a year, he tells himself that he won't be able to do it.

Mathilde has spent ages looking for where it all started – the beginning, the very beginning, the first clue, the first rift. She'd take things in reverse order, tracking backwards, trying to understand how it had happened, how it began. Each time she would come to the same point, the same date: that presentation one Monday morning at the end of September.

That meeting was where it all started, absurd though it may seem. Before that, there was nothing wrong. Before that everything was normal and went according to plan. Before that she had been deputy director of marketing in the main health and nutrition division of an international food company for more than eight years. She had lunch with her colleagues, went to the gym twice a week, didn't take sleeping pills, didn't cry in the metro or the supermarket and didn't pause for three minutes before she answered her children's questions. She went to work like everyone else and didn't throw up half the time when she got off the train.

So was one meeting all it took for everything to collapse?

That day she and Jacques were getting feedback from a well-known institute. They'd come to present the results of a study commissioned two months previously into the use of and attitudes to diet products. The methodology had been the subject of much internal debate, especially the prospective plan, on which major investment decisions depended. In the end they opted for two complementary approaches – qualitative and quantitative – which they had entrusted to the same company. Instead of appointing someone from the in-house team to take charge of the brief, Mathilde had decided to keep an eye on it herself. It was the first time they had worked with this particular institution, whose research methods were comparatively new. She had attended group meetings and face-to-face interviews, she'd tested the follow-up to the online questionnaire herself and asked to do some cross-tabulation of the data before they collated the results. She was pleased with how things had gone. She'd kept Jacques up to speed as she always did when they were working with a new partner.

First one date for the presentation had been set, then another, but Jacques had twice postponed at the last minute, claiming he had too much on. He absolutely insisted on being there. The size of the budget alone warranted his presence.

The day of the presentation, Mathilde arrived early to set up the room, check that the projector was working and that the coffee trays had been prepared. The director of the institute himself was going to present the results. Mathilde had invited the whole in-house team, the four product heads, the two researchers and the statistician.

They were all sitting round the table. Mathilde had exchanged a few words with the director of the institute. Jacques was late. Jacques was always late. Eventually he came in without offering any excuse. His features were drawn and he was badly shaved. Mathilde was wearing a dark suit and the pale silk blouse that she was fond of. She could recall it with strange precision. She also remembered how the man was dressed, the colour of his shirt, the ring he wore on his little finger, the pen sticking out of his jacket pocket, as though the most insignificant details had been inscribed on her memory, unbeknown to her, before she was aware of the importance of this moment, that something was about to happen that would be impossible to repair. After the usual formalities, the director of the institute began his presentation. He had total command of his subject – he hadn't just spent half an hour skimming through a document prepared by other people as often happened. He commented on the slides without notes, expressing himself with exceptional clarity. The man was both brilliant and charismatic. That was rare. He emanated a sort of conviction that commanded attention. That was immediately apparent from how attentive the team were to his every word and the absence of whispered remarks which normally plagued this sort of meeting.

Mathilde had noticed the man's hands, she remembered the expansive gestures which accompanied his words. She wondered where his light, almost imperceptible, accent was from, a particular inflection she couldn't identify. She very quickly sensed that the man was getting on Jacques's nerves, probably because he was younger and taller than him and at least his equal as a speaker. She quickly sensed Jacques bristle.

In the middle of the presentation Jacques had begun to show signs of impatience – he sighed ostentatiously and said 'yes, yes' aloud, intended to draw attention to the fact that the director was going too slowly or stating the obvious. Then he began looking at his watch in such a way that no one was in any doubt about his impatience. The team displayed no reaction; they knew his moods. Later, when the director was presenting the results of the quantitative study, Jacques expressed astonishment that their statistical significance didn't feature in the graphics on the screen. With somewhat exaggerated politeness, the director responded that only results whose statistical significance was above ninety-five per cent were shown. At the end of the presentation, Mathilde, who had commissioned the study, expressed her thanks for the work that had gone into it. It then fell to Jacques to say a few words. She turned to him, and as soon as she caught his eye she knew that Jacques would not be offering any thanks. In the past he'd impressed on her how important it was to establish relations of trust and mutual respect with outside contractors.

Mathilde asked the first questions about some points of detail before opening it up to the meeting.

Jacques was last to speak. With pinched lips and displaying the absolute self-confidence which she knew so well, he dismantled the study's recommendations one by one. He didn't question the reliability of the results, but the conclusions the institute had drawn from them. It was skilfully done. Jacques understood the market, brand identities and the history of his company inside out. But for all that, he was wrong.

Mathilde was used to agreeing with him. Firstly because they saw things in a similar way and secondly because it had struck her from the first months of working with him that agreeing with Jacques was a strategy that was both more comfortable and more effective. There was no point in confronting him. In fact, Mathilde always managed to express her reasons and her choices and sometimes got him to change his mind. But this time Jacques's attitude struck her as so unjust that she couldn't stop herself saying something. Presenting it as a suggestion so as not to contradict him directly, she explained how it seemed to her that the proposed direction with regard to the development of the market and the other studies carried out by the team were worth studying.

Jacques looked at her for a long time.

In his eyes, all she could read was surprise.

He didn't say anything else.

She concluded that her argument had won him over. She accompanied the director of the institute to the lift.

Nothing had happened.

Nothing serious.

It had taken her several weeks to return to that scene, to remember it in its entirety, to realise the extent to which every detail had remained in her memory – the man's hands, the lock of hair that fell across his forehead when he leaned forward, Jacques's face, what had been said, what had gone unspoken, the final minutes of the meeting, the way the man had smiled at her, his look of gratitude, the unhurried way he gathered up his things. Jacques had left the room without saying goodbye to him.

Later Mathilde had asked Éric how he thought things had gone. Was what she said hurtful, discourteous? Had she overstepped the mark? In a low voice Éric answered that she'd done something that day which none of the rest of them would have dared do and that was good.

Mathilde had gone back over the scene because Jacques's attitude towards her had changed, because nothing since had been as it was before, because it was then that the slow process of destruction that would take her months to recognise for what it was had begun.

But she always came back to this question: was that all it took for everything to collapse?

Was that all it took for her whole life to be subsumed in an absurd, invisible struggle which she could never win?

If it took her a long time to admit what was going on, the spiral they had embarked on, it was because up until then Jacques had always supported her. They had worked together from the start, defended their common positions, shared the same boldness, a certain taste for risk and the same refusal to take the easy option. She knew his tone better than anyone, the meaning of his gestures, his defensive laugh, his stance when he was in a strong position, his inability to give up, his upsets, his rages and his emotions. Jacques had the reputation of being a difficult character – he was known to be demanding, curt and unsubtle. People were scared of him and came to her more often than to him, but they recognised his competence. When Jacques recruited her she hadn't worked for three years. He chose her from the group of candidates that the HR department had selected. She was a single mother of three, a situation which up till then had brought her only rejections. She owed him for that. She got involved in working on the marketing plan, in major decisions about the product mix of each brand and in monitoring the competition. Gradually she began to write his speeches and take control of the management of a team of seven.

That day at the end of September, in the space of ten minutes, something had come tumbling down. Something had interfered with the precise high-performance mechanism which governed their relations, something she had neither seen nor heard. It began the same evening, when Jacques expressed surprise in front of several people at seeing her leave at six thirty, having apparently forgotten the numerous evenings she'd sacrificed to the company in order to prepare group presentations and the hours she'd spent at home finishing off reports.

And so a different mechanism was set in motion, a silent and inflexible one which wasn't going to stop until she cracked.

The first thing Jacques did was decide that the few minutes he spent with her each morning running through priorities and current projects was a waste of time. She'd just have to manage on her own and ask him if necessary. Likewise, he stopped coming to see her in her office at the end of the day, a ritual he had observed for years, a short break before going home. On more or less plausible pretexts, he avoided every opportunity to have lunch with her. He no longer consulted her on decisions and had stopped bothering about her opinion. He never again consulted her on anything at all.

Conversely, the following Monday he had turned up at the planning meeting she ran every week with the whole team, which he hadn't attended in ages. He sat across the table from her, as an observer, without a word to explain his presence, arms folded, sitting back in his chair. And he looked at her. From that first time, Mathilde felt ill at ease, because his look wasn't one of trust – it was a look that was judging her, seeking out a fault.

Then Jacques asked for copies of certain documents, took it into his head to have a look at the work of the researchers and product heads, to reread reports and to review resource allocation on various projects. Next, on several occasions he contradicted her in front of the team, looking as though he was suppressing some vague irritation or outright exasperation, and then in front of other people, during the regular exchanges they had with different department heads.

Then he had applied himself to systematically questioning her decisions, asking for details, demanding proof, justifications, figures to back up arguments. He began to express doubts and recriminations.

Then he started coming to her planning meeting every Monday.

Then he decided to chair it himself and as a result she could get on with something else.

She had thought that Jacques would come to his senses. That he would abandon his anger, let things get back to normal.

Things couldn't get out of control, become deadlocked like that over nothing. It was crazy.

She had tried not to alter her own attitude. She tried to bring off the projects she had been given, to maintain good relations with the team in spite of the uneasy feeling that had developed and was growing all the time. She had reckoned that time was what was needed, time for Jacques to get over it.

She hadn't reacted to any of his attacks – the ironic comments about her shoes or her new coat, the mean remarks about the dates of her Christmas holiday or the sudden illegibility of her handwriting; she had responded with patient, good-natured silence. She had responded with the faith she had in him.

Perhaps none of this had anything to do with her. Perhaps Jacques was going through a bad time and just needed to find his feet again, to get up to speed with projects he had long ago delegated. She had even imagined that he was ill, suffering from a secret disease that was silently eating away at him.

She refused to betray him and didn't complain about it to anyone. She kept quiet.

But Jacques continued in the same way, every day a little more irritated, distant and harsh.

Over time Mathilde had had to admit that whether Jacques was present or not, other people in the department didn't talk to her the way they used to, that they adopted an awkward, apologetic tone, since he wasn't far away. All except Éric, whose attitude to her hadn't changed.

In November Jacques forgot to invite her to an internal presentation of the ad campaign that the agency they used had produced for the launch of a new product. She found out about the meeting at the last minute from Jacques's secretary and rushed to the communications director's office. She knocked and found them both sitting on the leather sofa facing the flat-screen. Jacques didn't look at her, and the other man gave her only a vague acknowledgement. Neither of them got up or made space for her. Mathilde remained standing there with her arms folded the whole time, while they watched the three films over and over, comparing the images, the voice-overs and the editing. Neither Jacques nor the director of communications asked her opinion. They both behaved as though she had simply burst in by mistake and had no reason to be there.

That was the day she realised that Jacques's plan to destroy her was not confined to her own department, that he had begun discrediting her further afield and that it was completely within his power to do so.

For several weeks following that episode she asked for a meeting, through his secretary, and every time she passed him in the corridor or bumped into him at the coffee machine. Jacques always refused in an affable tone, putting it off or claiming he was too busy that week.

*

One day in November she burst into his office without knocking, closed the door behind her and demanded an explanation.

He had no idea what she was talking about. None whatsoever. Everything was absolutely normal. He was doing his job. End of story. She was well aware of the annual budget he was responsible for, the number of things he was involved in which depended on him. He didn't have time for her mood swings. He had better things to do with his time. The onus was on him to check and verify and take good decisions. She was a complicated person and she made everything else complicated too. What was the matter with her? Had she done something wrong? She probably needed a holiday. It had been a tough year. It was only natural she'd run out of steam. She was looking tense. Tired. No one was indispensable, she knew that. She just needed to take a few days off and she would see things more clearly.

She remembers his voice. It was a voice she didn't recognise. He could hardly suppress the hatred in it. It was a voice that left no possibility of going back to how things were before. It was a voice of condemnation.

From that day on, Jacques stopped talking to her.

*

Mathilde didn't take any time off. She stayed later and later at the office and began to work weekends. She behaved exactly as though she were guilty, as though she had a serious mistake to make up for or a need to prove herself. She had begun to feel tired, exhausted even. She felt as though she was working more slowly than before and less effectively. Little by little she had lost her sense of ease, her confidence. Several times Jacques cancelled business trips with her. He went by himself or replaced her at the last moment with someone else. He stopped telling her about his discussions with top management. He had begun forgetting to send her documents, to invite her to meetings, to copy her in on important emails. When she was away from her desk he would pile it with files bearing illegible instructions scribbled on Post-its. Then he decided to communicate with her only via the company intranet.

To that had been added a heap of insignificant little things of no importance which she could barely describe, which she wouldn't have been able to tell anyone about. The way he looked at her when they passed each other, the way he didn't look at her in the presence of others, the way he went ahead of her, the way he sat opposite her to observe her, and the way he'd started locking the door of his office when he left before her.

*

27

A collection of insidious, ridiculous little things which made her more isolated every day, because she hadn't been able to take stock of what was going on, because she hadn't wanted to raise the alarm. A pile of little things which added together had destroyed her sleep.

In the space of a few weeks Jacques had become someone else, someone she didn't know.

Because she has spent entire nights going over it hundreds of times, she is now able to put a name to what's happening to her. She's able to identify its different stages, where it began and where it's heading.
    But now it's too late.
    He wants her hide.

Light was coming in through the half-open curtains. Thibault was sitting on the edge of the bed, his body facing the room. For a few minutes he had been watching Lila sleep, her dishevelled hair, her open hands, her body rising and falling to the rhythm of her breathing. The alarm call still hadn't rung. Lila hadn't moved. Or else she had returned to that open, offered position in which he had observed her a few hours before.

He hadn't slept a wink. He had spent the rest of the night tossing and turning, with a feeling deep in his stomach that something was missing. They were unequal, both in sleep and in love.

The long silver chain descended between her breasts and then, with the weight of the pendant, dropped to the left: its heavy teardrop-shape rested on the sheets. Lila had this necklace from a previous love affair, but only ever hinted at its importance to her. Thibault moved closer to her shoulder and then her neck and breathed in deeply. One last time. The smell of her skin, the lingering trace of her perfume. Lila's face was smooth and peaceful. It was an expression he only saw when she was asleep. He brought his lips close to hers, as close as possible without brushing against them.

Then doubt crept in. What if he had been wrong right from the start? What if it was just a matter of finding the right rhythm, the right language? Perhaps she needed time. Perhaps she loved him silently, from a distance that only diminished by fits and starts. Perhaps that was her way of loving, the only way she was capable of. Perhaps there was no other proof but this: their bodies and their breathing, in harmony.

The alarm call had gone off. It was six o'clock. Lila opened her eyes and smiled. For a few seconds he held his breath.

Still lying on her back, she began to stroke the glans of his penis with the tips of her fingers, very gently, without taking her eyes off him. His penis became hard very quickly. He touched her cheek with his right hand, got up and went into the bathroom. When he came back into the bedroom, Lila was dressed and had tossed her things in her bag. She wanted to do her make-up before they left, so he went downstairs to settle the bill, then waited in the car with the windows down, repeating to himself that he could go through with it.

*

He remembered the November morning he had waited for her in vain at the taxi rank. The minutes before she contacted him, the twenty times he'd looked at his watch, her name eventually coming up on the screen of his mobile and the words she hadn't even taken the trouble to say aloud. They were supposed to be going to Prague for the weekend. He'd booked everything.

He remembered another time, one of those nights when he was aware how far away she was, sheltered in one of those private places he couldn't reach, how if he hadn't been there it wouldn't have mattered to her on the other side of the bed. He got dressed in silence. As he was putting his shoes on, she opened her eyes. He explained that he couldn't sleep, he was going home, it was nothing serious, and anyway nothing was serious in the end. She made a face. As he was leaving he took her face in his hands and looked at her. 'I love you, Lila,' he told her. 'I'm in love with you.'

She gave a start, exactly as though she had been slapped, and exclaimed, 'No, no.'

Maybe that was the day he understood that nothing could live or grow between them, that nothing could develop or deepen, and that they'd remain as they were, static, on the soft surface of love affairs that have fizzled out. Maybe that was when he told himself that one day he would have the strength to get himself out of this and never look back.

As it has every day for weeks, the alarm goes off just as Mathilde has managed to get back to sleep. She stretches out beneath the sheets.

This is the worst part: the moment of fear which begins anew every morning. Lying in bed and remembering what awaits her.

On Mondays the twins start school at eight, so she can't take her time. Mathilde gets up. Her body is exhausted. Exhausted even before she begins. Her body no longer recovers, it's emptied of its substance, its energy. Her body's become a dead weight.

She turns on the light, smooths the sheet with the flat of her hand, straightens the duvet. Her movements seem slow and clumsy to her, as though she has to think about each of them in order for them to happen at the right place at the right time. Yet five days a week she manages to get herself up, go to the bathroom, step into the bath and pull the shower curtain behind her. She lingers under the torrent of warm water. Often in the feeling of well-being that the shower brings she recovers the feelings of old, when her life flowed like water, when she was happy to go to work, when she had no more to worry about than choosing the suit or shoes she was going to wear.

She gives herself over to the memory of her body. That time seems long ago, gone for ever.

Now she would give anything to be able to close her eyes, to stop thinking, to stop knowing, to escape what awaits her.

How many times has she wished she could fall seriously ill? How many symptoms, syndromes, ailments has she imagined so that she could legitimately stay at home, legitimately say, 'I can't take any more'? How many times has she dreamed of going off with her sons, without any plans, leaving no forwarding address, setting off with all her savings? To leave her path and begin a new life somewhere else.

How many times has she thought that you could die of what she was going through, die of having to survive ten hours a day in a hostile environment?

As she's drying herself on the towel, she notices a dark mark on her left calf. She bends down and discovers a deep burn, three or four centimetres long. She straightens up and thinks. The night before she'd been frozen and had boiled some water to fill a hot water bottle, which she slipped into the bed before she went to sleep.

She must have fallen asleep like that with her skin stuck to the rubber. She's given herself a third-degree burn without realising. She looks again at the seeping wound. It's not going to get better by itself. Two months ago she broke her wrist when she fell on the stairs on the metro. After a week she resigned herself to going for an X-ray because she couldn't pick things up or hold on to them any more. The duty doctor held up her X-ray and told her off. Fortunately the fracture wasn't dislocated. To test spaghetti or green beans, she quickly dips her hand into boiling water. She doesn't feel anything. It's as though she is developing a sort of resistance to pain. She's getting tougher. She knows this when she looks at herself in the mirror. Her features have become so hollow. There's something closed about them, stretched to the extreme, which she can no longer undo.

Mathilde looks in the medicine cabinet for the plasters. She chooses the biggest one and sticks it on. It's ten past seven and she's got to make it. Get the breakfast ready, catch the metro, then the RER and get to work.

She's got to make it because she lives alone with three children, because they count on her to wake them up in the morning and they wait for her when they come home from school at the end of the day.

*

When she moved into this apartment, she sanded, repainted, put up shelves and bunk beds. She got on with things. She found a job, took the boys to the dentist, guitar lessons, basketball and judo.

She kept going.

Now they're older and she's proud of them, and of what she's rebuilt, this little island of peace whose walls are covered in drawings and photos, perched above the street. This little island where she's been able to introduce joy, to which joy has returned. Here all four of them have laughed, sung and played together. They've invented words and stories, made something that links them, joins them together. She's often thought that she's passed on to her children a kind of gaiety, a talent for joy. She's often thought that she has nothing more important to offer them than her laugh, beyond the infinite chaos of the world.

Now it's different. Now she's irritable and tired. It takes a superhuman effort for her to follow a conversation for more than five minutes, to be interested in what they're telling her. Sometimes she starts crying for no reason, when she's alone in the kitchen, when she watches them sleeping, when she stretches out in the silence. Now she feels sick to the heart when she gets out of bed; she scribbles what she's got to do on a

notepad, sticks useful instructions, dates and appointments to mirrors. So that she doesn't forget.

Now it's her sons who are protecting her, and she
knows that's not good. Théo and Maxime tidy their
room without being asked. They set the table, have
their shower and put their pyjamas on. They've done
their homework by the time she gets home and their
bags are ready for the next day. When Simon goes
out with his friends on a Saturday afternoon, he calls
her to tell her where he is, wants to know she's OK
with it and doesn't need him to get back sooner to look
after the twins. Maybe she'd like to go out for a bit,
to see friends or go to the cinema, he'll suggest. All
three of them watch her all the time, attentive to her
tone of voice, her moods, the hesitation in her movements. She can tell they're worried about her. They
ask her several times a day how she is. She talked to
them about it. At the beginning. She told them that
she had some problems at work, but they'd pass. Later
she tried to describe them, to explain the situation, the
way she had gradually fallen into a trap and how hard
it was to get herself out of it. With all the confidence
of a fourteen-year-old, Simon wanted to go and punch
Jacques right away, to slash the tyres of his car. He
demanded revenge. That had made her smile back
then, this adolescent revolt against the injustice done
to his mother. But can they really understand? They

don't know what business is, its constraints and mean tricks, the hushed conversations. They've never heard the noise the drinks dispenser makes, or the lift, or seen the grey carpet. They don't know about the superficial courtesy and the hidden resentments, the border skirmishes and the territorial battles, the secrets and the memos. Even for Simon, work is something abstract. And when she tries to translate things into a language they can understand – my boss, the woman who runs personnel, the man who looks after advertising, the big, big boss – it feels to her as though she might as well be telling them a story about barbarous Smurfs killing each other silently in a village cut off from the rest of the world.

She doesn't even talk about it to her friends.

In the beginning she tried to describe the glances, the delays, the excuses. She tried to describe the things that went unspoken, the suspicions, the insinuations. The avoidance strategies. The accumulation of petty irritations, covert humiliations, tiny things. She tried to describe how it all fitted together, how it came about. And every time the story seemed ridiculous, risible. And every time she would break off.

She'd end up dismissing it with a vague wave of her hand, as though all this didn't haunt her nights, didn't eat away at her little by little, as if none of it ultimately mattered.

She should have told someone.

At the start. Way back then.

When Jacques started saying to her in the morning in that tone of concern that he was so good at faking, 'You look dreadful.' Once, then twice, a few days apart. The third time he had used the word 'crap'. 'You look like crap.' But sounding vaguely worried.

What hate was contained in that word, hate she didn't want to hear.

She should have told someone about the time he had kept her waiting for forty-five minutes on some godforsaken industrial estate, ostensibly while he went to get the car, when the car park was only a couple of hundred yards away.

She should have told someone about the meetings cancelled at the last minute or relocated without telling her, the sighs, the sharp remarks under the guise of humour, and her calls which he no longer took, even when he was in his office.

Oversights, mistakes, irritations which, taken on their own, were just part of normal office life. Ridiculous incidents without any drama or fracas, which added together had ended up destroying her.

*

She thought she could resist.

She thought she could face up to it.

Little by little she got used to it without realising. She ended up forgetting how it had been before, even what her job was about. She ended up forgetting she used to work ten hours a day without looking up.

She hadn't realised that things could collapse like that, with no prospect of going back to how they were before.

She didn't know that a company could tolerate such violence, however surreptitious.

To permit this tumour to grow exponentially in its breast, without reacting or trying to cure it.

Often Mathilde thinks of that Ten-Can-Knockdown game which the boys love. They lay into those cans every year at the school fête, aiming at the bottom until the last of them tumble down.

Well, she's the target and today there's nothing left.

But when she thinks about it in the evenings, lying in bed or in the scalding water of the bath, she knows full well why she keeps silent.

She keeps silent because she's ashamed.

Mathilde opens the cupboard, grabs some knickers, trousers and a blouse. In the room next door, Simon's radio has come on. A few minutes later he knocks on the door and offers to wake up the twins. She glances at the time; she's doing OK. She goes into the kitchen, stops for a moment to think about what she has to do, the order she has to do things in. She doesn't switch on the old transistor. She's concentrating. Théo and Maxime burst in behind her and fling themselves at her for a kiss. Their bodies still have that night-time warmth. She strokes their sleep-crumpled faces and breathes in their smell. In the creases of their necks the arrangement of her own life seems simple to her. Her place is here beside them. Nothing else matters. She'll call the doctor, get him to come out, explain it to him. He'll examine her and agree that her body has no strength left, that there's nothing left – not an atom nor a wave. After he goes, she'll stay in bed till lunchtime and then she'll get up and go and do the shopping. Or she'll stay out all afternoon, filling herself with other people's noise, their colours and movements. She'll make a meal that the boys will love, in which everything's the same colour or every ingredient begins with the same letter. She'll make the table look nice, she'll wait for them to come home, she'll . . .

She'll call the doctor as soon as the boys have gone.

At the end of the table, half out of his seat, Théo has started talking. He's always been the chatty one; he knows dozens of jokes, funny stories, or sad ones, or ones that keep you up at night, scary stories. He's asking them to be quiet. This morning he's telling his brothers about a programme about the *Guinness Book of Records* that he saw a few days ago at a friend's house. Mathilde half listens at the start, watching the three of them. They're so beautiful. Théo and Maxime are ten. They're developing their own personalities. Simon's already taller than her. He's got his father's shoulders, the same way of sitting on the edge of a chair, off-balance. Their laughter brings her back to the conversation. They're talking about a man who holds the record for the number of bras he can undo one-handed in one minute. And another one who in the same amount of time can put his pants on and take them off again eighty times.

'Tell us some more feats!' shouts Maxime in a state of high excitement. Théo goes on. There's a man who can tie a knot in cherry stalks with his tongue, and one who catches Smarties between two sticks. The other two burst out laughing simultaneously. Mathilde interrupts them to point out that these are not really feats and asks them to think about what these people are actually doing: don't they think that there's something humiliating in taking your pants off and putting them back on dozens of times to become the world champion in your category? They think about it and nod. And then Théo adds in all seriousness: 'Yes, but the guy who cuts bananas in two with his hand, just like that, skin and all, that's a real feat, isn't it, Mum?'

Mathilde strokes Théo's cheek and laughs.

And then they laugh too, all three of them, astonished to hear her laugh.

For weeks, in the morning light, as they sit round the kitchen table, hoping to hear her voice, searching her face for the smile that's no longer there, she has felt as though her sons are looking at her like she were a time bomb.

But not today.

Today's the twentieth of May, and all three of them

have gone off, bags and satchels on their backs, reassured and calm.

Today's the twentieth of May, and she's started the day by laughing.

Lila put her bag in the boot and got into the car beside him. Before he pulled off, Thibault called in to say he'd be starting his shift half an hour late. Rose said that they'd cope with the doctors they had. It hasn't got crazy yet.

They drove in silence. After an hour Lila fell asleep, her head against the window and a fine trickle of saliva running from her mouth to the top of her neck.

He reflected that he loved her, loved everything about her, her fluids, her substance, her taste. He felt as though he had never loved in this way, with this constant feeling of loss, with this feeling that nothing could be foreseen, nothing could be held on to.

On the outskirts of Paris the traffic got heavier. A few miles from the ring road, they almost came to a standstill. Stuck behind a lorry, he relived each moment of last night's dinner. He could see himself leaning across the table, his body inclining forward, reaching towards her. And Lila sitting back in her chair, distant as always. He could see himself and the way he had sunk in little by little, trying to give the right answers to the questions she kept asking – what are you looking for? What do you want? What do you need ideally, and what if . . .? A barrage of questions so that she didn't have to say anything about herself, about what she was seeking, so as not to disturb her own silence.

Him, trying to look good, be funny and witty and nice and relaxed.

Him, his mystery removed, stripped bare.

Him, a fly trapped under a glass.

He had forgotten how vulnerable he was. Was that what being in love meant, this feeling of fragility? This fear that you could lose everything at any time, through a slip or a wrong answer or an unfortunate word? Was this uncertainty about oneself the same at forty as at twenty? And if so, was there anything more pitiful, more vain?

Outside her place he turned off the engine. Lila woke up. He leaned over to kiss her. He slid his tongue into her mouth. One last time. He laid his hand on her breast, the fingers outstretched. He stroked her skin in the place he loved so much and then he said: 'I want us to stop seeing each other. I can't go on like this, Lila, I can't. I'm tired.'

The words were unbearably banal. Clichés that added insult to injury. But they were all he had.

Lila got up and opened the door. She went round the back of the car to the boot and then came back, with her bag over her shoulder. She leaned down and said, 'Thanks.'

And then after a moment, 'Thanks for everything.'

There was neither pain nor relief in her expression. She went into her building without looking back.

He had done it.

He let Rose know that he was on call and she gave him his first address over the phone: high fever, flu symptoms. She called back a few minutes later to ask if he could handle sector six in addition to four. Frazera had broken his wrist the previous night and the fracture was displaced. The controller hadn't yet found a doctor to replace him.

Thibault said yes.

He's just parked in an unloading bay outside a building where he's expected. He looks at his phone. He knows what he's hoping for. He knows that all day he's going to be looking at his mobile, waiting for the SMS symbol. His appointments used to be managed by radio. Now, for reasons of confidentiality, the emergency services have a set of mobile phones and a speed-dialling system. Every time the base sends him a new address he can't help hoping to see Lila's name. For weeks, that sound is going to torment him.

He hopes she'll miss him, just like that, all of a sudden. A dizzying void that she can't ignore. He hopes that as the hours go by she'll be overtaken by doubts, that little by little she'll come to realise what his absence means. He wants her to realise that no one will ever love her as he does, beyond the limits she imposes through her fundamental solitude, which she erects against everything around her but never mentions out loud.

It's ridiculous. *He*'s ridiculous. Grotesque. Who does he think he is? What makes him think he's exceptional and superior?

Lila won't come back. She'll accept what he said. Right now she'll be celebrating this outcome: nice and easy, served up on a plate. She knows that people who love you more than you can love them back end up being a burden.

He's going to see his first patient. He leaves Lila's perfume still floating in the air, the car windows half open.

'You have to pull out the drip,' Frazera told him one evening. He's a specialist in breaks, and not just of the wrist. They'd got together for a drink after a long weekend when they'd both been on call. Helped by the warm wave of vodka spreading through his veins, Thibault had talked to him about Lila: his feeling of embracing something insubstantial that crumbled away. That feeling of closing his arms on emptiness, a dead gesture.

Frazera told him he should get out right away, make a strategic withdrawal. And with a faraway look at the bottom of his glass he concluded: 'In every passionate relationship there is a kind of savagery that's in-built and inexhaustible.'

Thibault's in his car outside a nondescript apartment building. He looks at his phone one last time in case he missed the beep.

He's done it. He's done it at last: pulled out the drip.
He's done it and he can be proud of himself.

She smiled. As though she was expecting it. As if she'd had ages to get used to the idea.
She said thanks. Thanks for everything.
Is it possible to be so blind to someone else's despair?

As the door closes behind her, Mathilde reaches into her bag until her hand touches metal. She's always afraid that she's forgotten something – her keys, her phone, her purse, her travelcard.

She wasn't like that before. Then she was never afraid. Then she felt light, she didn't need to check. Objects didn't escape her attention. They possessed coordinated motion, natural and fluid. Back then, objects didn't slide off the furniture, didn't get knocked over, didn't get in her way.

She didn't make the call. Since her GP retired, she hasn't had a family doctor. Just as she was on the point of calling the number she found on the Internet it seemed to her that it was pointless. She isn't ill. She's tired. Like hundreds of people she passes every day. So by what right, on what pretext, could she call out someone she doesn't know? She wouldn't have known how to tell him. To say simply: I can't go on. And shut her eyes.

*

She takes the stairs. On the staircase she passes Mr Delebarre, her downstairs neighbour who comes up twice a week to complain the boys are making too much noise. Even when they're not there. Mr Delebarre puts on his exhausted look and gives her a feeble greeting. Mathilde doesn't stop. Her hand slides down the banister, her feet are silent on the plush carpet. Today she doesn't want to spend a few minutes being pleasant, keeping up a conversation. She doesn't want to remember that Mr Delebarre is widowed and alone and ill, that all he's got to do is listen to the noise coming from upstairs, exaggerating or even inventing it. She doesn't want to imagine Mr Delebarre adrift in the silence of his big apartment.

She knows herself. She knows where that will lead. She always has to look for excuses, explanations, reasons to be indulgent towards other people. She always ends up finding that people have good reasons for being the way they are. But not today. Oh no. Today she would like to be able to tell herself that Mr Delebarre is an idiot. Because today is 20 May. Because something is going to happen. Because things can't go on as they are. The price is too high. The price to be paid for having a swipe card for clocking in, a card for the canteen, an insurance card, a three-zone metro card, the price to be paid for taking part in the onward rush of life.

*

In the cool morning air, Mathilde walks along the side of the garden in the middle of the square. At this hour of the day the streets seem washed clean, renewed. In the distance she can hear a dustcart. Mathilde looks at her watch and hurries up; her heels click on the pavement.

As soon as she gets to the metro platform she notices it's unusually crowded. People are standing bunched together, but without crossing the rubber strip that marks the limit beyond which it is dangerous to go. The few seats provided are taken, there's something both gloomy and febrile in the air. Mathilde looks up at the digital display. The waiting times for the next trains have been replaced by two bright lines. The sound of a female voice suddenly invades the platform: 'Due to a technical fault, the Mairie de Montreuil service is seriously delayed.'

Anyone who uses public transport regularly masters its peculiar language – its subtleties, its idioms and its grammar. Mathilde knows the different scenarios and their probable impact on her journey time. A 'technical failure', a 'signalling problem', a 'timetable adjustment' mean moderate delays. More worryingly, a 'passenger taken ill' means that someone somewhere in another station has fainted, pulled the emergency alarm or has had to be evacuated. A passenger taken ill can seriously affect the flow of trains. And much more worryingly, a 'serious passenger incident', a term commonly reckoned to indicate a suicide, can paralyse traffic for several hours. People need to be evacuated.

Every four days in Paris a man or woman jumps in front of a train. Mathilde read it in the paper. The authorities are discreet about the exact figures, but there have long been psychological support services for drivers who are affected. Some of them never get over it. They are declared unfit for work, reassigned to ticket counters or the back office. On average, a driver encounters a suicide attempt at least once in his career. Do people in cities commit suicide more than elsewhere? She's often wondered about that, without going to the trouble of finding out the answer.

For the past few months, when Mathilde is on her way home from work, she has found herself watching the tracks, fixing her gaze on them, staring at the stones that cover the ground, the depth of the hole. Sometimes she feels her body inclining forward, almost imperceptibly, her exhausted body seeking rest.

Then she thinks of Théo, Maxime and Simon, their images superimposed on top of all the others, bright and moving, and Mathilde steps back, moves away from the edge.

*

She tries to carve out a space for herself amid the crowd. You have to earn your place, your territory. You have to respect the order of arrival and observe the minimum distance between people, which shrinks as the platform fills up.

There's no train announced.

She'll miss the 8.45, and the 9.00, and even the 9.15. She's going to be late. And by complete chance, Jacques will be standing in front of the lift when she gets out or waiting at her office door. He will have been looking for her everywhere and won't have kept quiet about it – even though he hasn't said a word to her for three weeks – he'll be looking at his watch, with a frown and a doubtful expression. Because Jacques watches her timekeeping closely, her absences, he's on the lookout for slip-ups. Because he lives a five-minute drive from the office and couldn't give a damn about the journey she makes every day like most of the employees on site, nor the number of external factors that could prevent her from being on time.

For the moment, her aim is to stay in the right place on the platform: not to let herself be dragged to the back, to hold her position. When the train comes, it'll be packed full of irascible people. She's going to have to fight. According to an unwritten law, a form

54

of underground legal precedent that has applied for decades, those who are first remain first. Anyone who tries to flout this law finds himself being heckled. In the distance there's a grumbling, a vibration that sounds like the long-awaited train. But the tunnel remains dark and empty. The electronic display still gives nothing away. The female announcer is silent. It's hot. Mathilde looks at the others, men and women, their clothes, their shoes, their hair, the shape of their buttocks. She looks at them from the back, from the front and in profile. You've got to do something. When she catches someone's eye, she looks away. Even when it's busy, there remains on public transport both a certain intimacy and a sense of reserve; limits imposed on the eye since they can't be imposed on the body. So Mathilde looks at the platform opposite. It's almost empty.

On the other side the trains are running normally, one after another in their regular rhythm. There's no point trying to find an explanation. In the opposite direction people are getting on the metro and arriving at work on time.

Finally Mathilde is aware of a rumbling sound to her left that grows ever louder. Heads turn expectantly, impatiently. At last! It's time to take a deep breath, flatten your bag against your hip and check that it's closed properly. The train slows and stops. It's here. It disgorges, regurgitates, releases its flood. Someone shouts: 'Let people off.' There's shoving, trampling. It's war. Every man for himself. Suddenly it's a matter of life or death, getting on this one and not having to wait for the next one, which may never come, not risking getting to work even later. 'For fuck's sake! Let people off!' The crowd parts grudgingly. You mustn't lose sight of the door, you have to stay near it, not let yourself get dragged back by the sheer number of people. You have to position yourself to one side, close to the door. Suddenly the horde surges forward, getting ahead of her, she's not going to make it. The carriage is already full, there's not a square inch left. However, she knows that she can get in. She'll have to force her way. She'll have to stretch her arm out, grab the pole in the middle, ignoring the cries and protests, and hold tight and pull. Pull with all her might to propel her body inside. They'll just have to budge up. In the face of her determination, they yield.

The signal indicating that the doors are about to close sounds. Apart from her right arm, which is sticking out, she's almost there. The door judders shut, indifferent to the groans and protestations.

Mathilde gains an inch or so with her left foot, pushes one last time and she's in.

*

56

On the platform the female voice is announcing that trains are running normally again on line 9.

It's all a matter of perspective.

At the following stations, Mathilde gets deeper into the carriage, gains a few extra inches, hangs on so as not to have to get off.

You mustn't give an inch.

The air is heavy. Bodies have fused together in a single compacted, harassed mass. Remarks have given way to silence, everyone is silently resigned to their fate, chins raised to the open windows, hands seeking support.

Then Mathilde thinks that this too is how 20 May begins, with this miserable, absurd struggle. Nine stations to get through, nine suffocating stations, torn from the fever of a morning of crowds, nine stations of struggling for air surrounded by people who only use a bar and a half of soap a year.

Suddenly a woman starts making strange sounds, high-pitched and progressively more drawn out. It's not a cry nor a groan, more like a wail. She is holding on to the central pole, pressed between a generous bust and a rucksack. The sound that is coming from the woman's mouth is unbearable. People turn round, observing her. They exchange perplexed glances.

The woman is looking for someone who can help her. Mathilde manages to extricate her hand and put it on her arm. They look at each other. She smiles at her.

The woman stops wailing. She's breathing loudly, her face twisted in fear.

'Aren't you feeling well?'

As soon as she asks the question Mathilde realises how stupid it is. The woman doesn't answer. She's making a superhuman effort not to scream. She's breathing more and more loudly. She begins to wail again and then this time she screams. Comments start up on all sides, at first in low voices and then more audibly. What's she thinking of, taking the metro on a day when there are technical problems, if she's claustrophobic? Make her get off. Oh no, for God's sake, don't pull the emergency cord. We're not out of the woods.

The woman is a disruptive element, a human failure capable of holding up the trains.

Mathilde's hand is still on the woman's arm. She's trying to smile.

'I'll get off with you at the next station. It'll only be a few seconds. See, the train's slowing down.'

The train stops, the doors open and Mathilde goes ahead of the woman to clear a passage. Please. Push. Let her through. She's holding on to the woman's sleeve.

She looks to see which station they're at. On the platform, below the sign that says Charonne, she makes her sit down. The woman seems to be calming down and Mathilde offers to go and get some water or something to eat from the vending machine. The woman starts to get agitated again. She's going to be late, she mustn't be, she can't get back on the train, she's only just found a job through a temp agency. Yes, she's claustrophobic but she usually copes. She thought she was going to manage it.

And then the woman starts breathing more loudly, gasping quicker and quicker. She's trying to get air, her limbs seem shaken by tremors, her hands are clutching each other in a manner she can't control.

Mathilde asked for help and someone went up to the ticket office. A man from the transport authority in a blue-green suit has come down. He's rung the fire brigade. The woman can't stand up. Her whole body is tensed up and being shaken by jolts. She's still breathing noisily.

They wait.

The platform is packed. The transport officials have created a security cordon. There are now three or four of them. All around, people form little groups, craning their necks.

Mathilde wants to scream. She sees herself in the woman's place, their images superimposed; for a brief moment they are one and the same person, swallowed by the neon signs, huddled up by the snack machines.

And then Mathilde looks around her. And she thinks that all these people, every last one of them, one day or another will be sitting here, or somewhere like it, unable to move. The day they collapse.

He'd gone down to the metro to respond to a panic attack at Charonne station. The fire brigade had passed on the call to his base; they were swamped because of a big fire in the area. Rose put out a general call. Thibault was a few streets away, so he stopped off there.

A woman of around thirty was sitting on the platform hyperventilating. By the time he got there, she was starting to calm down. A crowd had gathered around her, giving curious glances, peering to see better. The crowd didn't miss any of the performance. Two people managed to help her to the office behind the ticket counter where Thibault was able to administer a sedative. The woman's breathing returned to normal, her hands unclasped. He was double-parked so he couldn't stay. A metro official promised he would get her to a taxi when she felt better.

At a red light he looks around: people walking quickly, coming out of the metro in groups, running across the street; people queuing at ATMs, smoking outside buildings or cafés. So many people he cannot count, all subject to the city's flow, its speed; unaware they're being watched, seen from a distance, at street corners, an infinite number of fragile identities which he cannot grasp as a whole. From behind the windscreen, Thibault watches women; they've started wearing light clothes: floaty dresses, short skirts, sheer tights. Bare legs sometimes. The way they carry their bags by the handle or with the strap over their shoulder, the way they walk without noticing anyone or wait for the bus with a faraway look.

Suddenly the girl who joined his school in his last year comes into his mind. He had carved her name on a desk. She was from Caen. Or was it Alençon? He's thinking about that girl now. Her fine hair. Her riding boots and her boyish appearance. It's odd, thinking of that girl now. He was in love with her. Or with her reflection in other people's eyes. They didn't talk to each other. They had different circles of friends. Thinking of that girl, more than twenty years on . . . saying to yourself: that was twenty years ago. And then counting up to twenty-five. It was twenty-five years ago. Back when his left hand still had five fingers.

It was twenty-five years ago. That sounded like a

typing error, a bad joke. Can you say that without falling off your chair: 'It was twenty-five years ago'?

He's left Lila. He's done it. And that statement contains something that sounds like an achievement, a feat.

And yet the wound of love contains within it all silences, abandonments, regrets, all of which in the course of the years adds up to a generic sort of pain. And a confused one. Yet the wound of love promises nothing; not after, not elsewhere.

His life is diffracted. From a distance it seems to possess unity and direction. You can recount it, describe his days, the division of his hours and weeks, follow his movements. His address is known, so are the habits he's trying to break, the days he goes to the supermarket, the evenings when all he can do is listen to music. But close up, his life looks confused, it splits into fragments, there are pieces missing.

From close up, he's just a Playmobil figure slotted into his car, his hands clutching the steering wheel, a little plastic character who has lost his dream.

The station manager had said that a doctor would be there any minute. Another train was rumbling in from the left. Mathilde didn't wait. She was late enough as it was. She left the woman on her seat; other people were looking after her. She seemed a bit less tensed-up but she still couldn't stand. The woman said thank you. Mathilde got on the metro. She forced her way and wedged her back against a flip-up seat. She was in a good position. At Nation she got off and made her way through the impatient crowd. She took the passage that led to line 1. Here trains seemed to be running normally. She waited less than a minute for the next train, then she got off at the gare de Lyon.

Now Mathilde is heading for the RER. She doesn't look at the time. She knows by heart the corridors, the stairs, the shortcuts of this underground world, woven like a web in the bowels of the city. For eight years Mathilde has been using the same long tunnel that goes under the station to get to line D; here every day several thousand people's paths criss-cross: two columns of insects, disgorged in waves on to the slippery tiled floor, a rapid two-way street whose rhythms and cadences have to be respected. Bodies brush against one another, or avoid contact or sometimes collide in a strange sort of choreography. Here a vast exchange between the inside and the outside takes place, and between the city and its suburbs. Here people are in a hurry, they walk quickly: 'We're going to work, madam.'

Mathilde used to be one of the fastest; she'd pull out on the left with a confident, conquering stride. She used to get annoyed when the flow slowed. She'd curse the slowcoaches. Today she's one of them; she's well aware that she can't keep up the pace any more, she drags herself along, no longer has the energy. She sags.

At the other end of the tunnel, at the foot of the escalators, the automatic gates mark the entrance to the RER. You have to get your ticket or travelcard out and cross the border. In this even lower indeterminate zone you can buy a croissant or a newspaper, drink a coffee standing up.

To reach platforms 1 and 3 you have to go lower still, sink into the bowels of the city. Here the local and national railway companies share the territory. The traveller on line D doesn't know what belongs to whom. He slips through this common perimeter zone as best he can. At this point of intersection, interconnection, he feels his way, like a hostage left to his own devices between two worlds.

Like everyone else, Mathilde has learnt over the years the rudiments of another language, she has acquired new reflexes for the sake of her health, accepted the elementary rules necessary for survival. The trains have names consisting of four capital letters displayed on the front of the engine. The name of the train is known as its 'code'.

To get to work, Mathilde always catches the RIVA, which goes to Melun. This is not some sleek mahogany boat or the promise of a further shore. Just a noisy rain-smeared train. If she misses that, she takes the ROVO or the ROPO. But if she gets on a BIPE, RIPE or ZIPE by mistake, it's a disaster: those trains go non-stop all the way to Villeneuve-Saint-George. And the NOVO doesn't stop before Maisons-Alfort. The problem stems from the fact that they all use the same track.

Blue screens, suspended overhead like televisions in hospital, show a list of the next trains, their final destination, the time they're expected and how late they're running. The delay can be measured in minutes case by case or else by the message 'train delayed' flashing on all the lines. That's a very bad sign. Electronic signs, which are older, are situated in different parts of the platform. They content themselves with announcing the destination of the next departure and its stops, indicated by a white square. To these different sources of information are added a certain number of random announcements, delivered by a computerised voice. Which generally contradicts the screens and the signs. If the loudspeakers announce a ROPO, it's not unusual for the platform signs to be predicting the arrival of a RIPE.

The traveller on line D consequently receives a number of contradictory injunctions. With a little experience, he learns to sort through them, to seek confirmation, to consider different eventualities in order to come to a decision. The novice, the one-off traveller who finds himself there by chance, looks around, panics and asks for help.

Mathilde looks like the kind of person who gets asked for information. People have always stopped her in the street, rolled down their windows when she passes, come up to her looking embarrassed.

It's half past nine. The doors of a ROVO shut in her face so she'll have to wait for the next train, in a quarter of an hour. At the end of the platform the predominant smell is urine, but it's the only place you can sit down. She's tired. Some days when she's listening for the sound of the train, her buttocks stuck to the orange plastic, she wonders deep down whether it wouldn't be better to spend the whole day in the bowels of the earth, let the useless hours flow by, and around lunchtime go up a level to buy a sandwich, then go back down and resume her place. Remove herself from the flow, the movement.

Give in.

The ROPO arrived. She hesitated for a second and then went into the carriage. Once seated she closed her eyes and didn't open them again till the train came back up to ground level. The weather was bright.

Eight minutes later, at Vert-de-Maisons, she got out of the carriage and went towards the main exit, a bottleneck where a line of travellers soon built up, like at the supermarket checkout. She waited her turn, then filled her lungs with the outside air.

Mathilde takes the stairs, goes into the tunnel under the tracks and comes out again at street level.

She's been making the same journey for eight years, the same steps every day, the same turnstiles, the same underground passages, the same glances at clocks; each day her hand reaches out in the same place to hold or push the same doors, touches the same rails.

Exactly the same.

Just as she's leaving the station, it seems that she's reached her own limit, her saturation point beyond which it's impossible to go. It feels as though each of her actions, each of her movements, because they have been repeated three thousand times, threatens her balance.

Though she has lived for years without thinking about it, today this repetition seems to her like a sort of violence being done to her body, a silent sort of violence capable of destroying her.

Mathilde is over an hour late. She doesn't hurry, doesn't quicken her step. She doesn't phone ahead to say she's almost there. No one could care less anyway. Little by little, Jacques has managed to take away from her all the important projects she was working on, to distance her from any issues, to reduce her involvement with the team to a minimum. Through a lot of reorganisation and redefinition of assignments and responsibilities, he has managed in the space of a few months to strip her of everything that constituted her job. Under increasingly obscure pretexts, he has succeeded in excluding her from meetings that would have kept her in the loop or enabled her to get involved in other projects. In early December, Jacques sent her an email to tell her that she absolutely had to take the two days' holiday that she hadn't used that year. The day before she went, he arranged an impromptu drinks party for the whole floor the next day. He postponed the date of her annual appraisal ten times and eventually announced that it would not be happening, without offering any explanation.

In the street parallel to the railway line, Mathilde has stopped. She turns to the light long enough to feel the sun on her face, to let its warmth bathe her eyes and hair.

It's gone ten when she goes through the door of the Brasserie de la Gare.

It's gone ten and she couldn't give a damn.

Bernard, with a dishcloth over his shoulder, gives her a broad smile: 'So, young lady, we didn't see you on Friday for the Loto . . .'

Now she's playing the lottery twice a week, reading her horoscope in *Le Parisien* and going to see clairvoyants.

'I took a day off to go on my son's school trip to the chateau of Versailles. The teacher needed volunteers.'

'Was it good?'

'The rain never stopped.'

Bernard groans in sympathy and turns to the coffee machine.

Mathilde takes a table. Today's the twentieth of May, so she's not going to drink it standing up. Today, on the twentieth of May, she is going to sit down, because it has taken her over an hour and a half to get here and she's wearing three-inch heels.

She's going to sit down because no one's waiting for her, because she no longer serves any purpose.

Bernard puts the cup in front of her, pulls out the chair on the other side of the table.

'Bit off-colour this morning, eh?'

'Bit off-colour every morning.'

'No! Last week when you came in with your light floaty dress, it was like spring was in the air! Isn't that right, Laurent? It's spring, Mathilde, you'll see, and the world keeps turning like the hem of a flowery dress.'

Nice people are the dangerous ones. They threaten the whole structure, shake the fortress. One more word from Bernard, and Mathilde might burst into tears. Bernard's gone back behind his counter. He's bustling about, giving her the occasional wink or smile. The café's almost empty at this time. He's preparing the sandwiches and *croque-monsieurs* for the lunchtime rush. He's humming a song that she knows without being able to name it, one of those love songs about memories and regrets. The regulars, leaning on the counter and staring into space, are listening in religious silence.

*

Mathilde rummages in her bag for her purse. No luck. Suddenly, in irritation, she tips its contents out on the table. Among the objects in front of her – keys, travel-sickness pills, lipstick, eyeshadow, packets of tissues, luncheon vouchers – she discovers a white envelope on which she recognises Maxime's writing: 'For Mum'. She tears it open. Inside she sees one of those cards that are all the rage in the playground, which her sons regard as priceless and are sold in packets of five or ten. Cards which they use in their battles throughout the day and spend their time swapping. Mathilde begins by unfolding the little note that accompanies the card. In careful handwriting, without any spelling mistakes, her son has written: 'Mum, I want you to have my Argent Defender card, it's very rare, but that's OK, I've got two of them. You'll see, it's a hero card that protects you all your life.'

The Argent Defender is wearing sumptuous shining armour. He stands out against a dark turbulent background. He's holding a sword in his left hand and in the other he brandishes an immaculate shield at an unseen enemy. The Argent Defender is handsome and noble and brave. He's not afraid.

Under the picture you can read the number of points he is worth, as well as a short text summarising his vocation: 'Our cause is to fight swiftly and mercilessly against any element of evil that surfaces in Azeroth.'

Mathilde smiles.

On the back, against an ochre background covered in opaque clouds, the name of the game is written in Gothic script: World of Warcraft.

A few days ago, Théo and Maxime explained to her that Pokémon and Yu-Gi-Oh cards, which had been swallowing up their pocket money for months, were now old hat. Past it. Relegated to the cupboard. Now *everybody* had World of Warcraft cards and *nobody* played with anything but that. Not having any WoW cards, her sons were left out, nobodies, charity cases.

Last Saturday, Mathilde bought them each two packets. They were beside themselves with joy. They did some swaps with each other, decided their attack and defence strategies and trained all day for their forthcoming combats. Virtual combats conducted on the ground in the playground, which she couldn't make head or tail of.

Mathilde slips the Argent Defender into her jacket pocket. The card has given her the courage to get up. She leaves the money on the table, puts her things back in her bag, gives Bernard a wave and leaves.

*

A few hundred yards further on, she stumbles, catches herself, puts the other foot forward. The least breath of wind, the smallest dizzy spell, could make her collapse. She has reached the point of fragility, of disequilibrium, at which things lose their meaning, their proportion. With this degree of vulnerability, the tiniest detail is capable of engulfing her in joy or destroying her.

A woman of about fifty in a velvet dressing gown opened the door to him. As soon as she saw Thibault, her expression brightened.

'You again!'

Neither the address, nor the place, let alone the woman's face, were familiar to him.

'Sorry?'

'You were the one who called a fortnight ago.'

He let it go. He thought that the woman must have confused him with another doctor. He followed her in, looking around as he went. The sideboard in the living room, the porcelain knick-knacks, the thick curtains in the bedroom, didn't look familiar either. Nor did this woman's thin body, her pink nylon nightdress, or her long painted nails. After he listened to her chest, Thibault asked if she had kept her last prescription so that he'd know what treatment she'd been prescribed. The headed paper she showed him had his name on it. He spent a few seconds looking at the prescription, with his own writing on it and the date – 8 May – when he had indeed done a 7 a.m. to 7 p.m. shift.

During a shift it's not unusual for him to see two or three patients he knows. But normally he can remember them.

The woman had all the symptoms of a secondary bronchial infection. He wrote out a new prescription with his right hand, as he has done for years, although he is left-handed. He looked around one last time. Hand on heart – what was left of it – he could have sworn that he had never before set foot in this apartment. Yet he'd been there twelve days previously.

He has only eight fingers. Five on one hand and three on the other. That is part of him, the missing part, a thing defined by its absence. It's a moment of his life, a date, an approximate time. A moment inscribed on his body. Or rather subtracted from it. It happened one Saturday night at the end of his second year as a medical student.

Thibault was studying at Caen. He went home to his parents one weekend a month. He used to meet his old school friends for a drink and then they'd go to the Marechalerie, a disco about twenty miles from home. Four or five of them would pile into Pierre's van. They'd drink spirits at the bar, dance a bit, look at the girls. That evening he and Pierre had had an argument about nothing, and then things had escalated, something that went back a long way had come up out of nowhere. He was studying medicine and Pierre had failed his bac. He was living in Caen and Pierre was working in his father's garage. Girls liked him; they noticed his fine hands. Pierre was well over six foot and weighed about nineteen stone. Pierre was dead drunk. He had pushed Thibault several times. He was shouting above the music: 'I don't give a fuck about your pretty-boy face and your nice family.' People cleared a space around them. They were asked to leave. Around three in the morning, they got into the van. Thibault sat in the passenger seat, the two others were in the back. Pierre was still outside, furious and refusing to get behind the wheel until Thibault got out. Till he beat it. Till he pissed off. He'd just have to walk home. The door on Thibault's side was open. Pierre stood there and demanded that he get out. They argued back and forth for a few more minutes, the voices of the two others protesting above theirs. At exactly the same moment they both gave in. Thibault put his hand on the door frame to get out just as Pierre slammed the door shut with incredible force. The van shook. Thibault cried out. His hand was trapped and the door was jammed. Each of them in turn pulled, rattled and kicked it. Inside, Thibault was struggling not to lose consciousness. He didn't know how long they stayed like that, panicky and confused, their movements slowed by alcohol, insults being fired off on all sides, and him, alone in the cab, his hand held fast by the metal. Half an hour, an hour, maybe more. Perhaps he fainted. When they managed to get it open, Thibault's hand was literally crushed flat and two of his fingers were hanging loose at the point where they joined his hand. They drove to the nearest town. In the hospital they waited for the duty surgeon.

The two fingers no longer had any blood-flow and were too badly damaged for an operation to repair or reattach them. A few days later, the ring finger and pinkie on his left hand had to be amputated. Two dead and swollen things of which there would remain no trace but a smooth white surface above the palm.

His dream had been cut short. Cleanly. His dream lay at the bottom of a bin in a provincial hospital whose name he had never forgotten. He would never be a surgeon.

After his time as a house officer, Thibault began as a locum for the doctor in the village where he had grown up, one week per month and two months in the summer. The rest of the time he worked for a home-help network. When Dr M. died, Thibault took over his practice.

He did consultations in the morning in his consulting room and devoted the afternoons to house calls. He covered an area with a fifteen-mile radius, paid off his student loan and went to lunch at his parents' on a Sunday. In the village of Rai in the Orne region, he became a respectable man whom people greeted at the market and invited to join the Rotary Club, a man who was addressed as Doctor and to whom girls from good families were introduced.

Things could have gone on like that, followed their course along the dotted line. He could have married Isabelle, the lawyer's daughter, or Élodie, the daughter of the Groupama insurance agent in the neighbouring town. They would have had three children. They would have extended his waiting room, repainted, bought a people carrier and found a locum so they could go away for the summer.

Things would probably have been nicer.

After four years, Thibault sold the practice. He put some belongings in a case and caught the train.

He wanted the city, its movement, the heavy air at the day's end. He wanted the bustle and the noise.

He began working for Paris Medical Emergencies, at first doing relief cover, then as a temp, then as a partner. He continued to come and go, here and there, according to the patients' calls and his shifts. He never left.

*

Perhaps he has nothing else to give but a prescription written in blue pen on the corner of a table. Perhaps all he will ever be is someone who passes through and leaves.

His life is here. Even though none of it fools him. Not the music that comes through windows, nor the illuminated signs, nor the bursts of voices around television sets on evenings when there's football on. Even if he has known for a long time that the singular trumps the plural and how fragile conjunctions are.

His life is in his crappy Renault Clio, with its empty plastic bottles and crumpled Bounty wrappers on the floor.

His life is in this incessant toing and froing, these exhausted days, these stairways, these lifts, these doors which close behind him.

His life is at the heart of the city. And the city, with its noise, covers the complaints and the murmurs, hides its poverty, displays its dustbins and its wealth, and ceaselessly increases its speed.

The glittering tower rose up before her in the spring light, a strip of cloud reflected in its glass sides. The sun seems filtered from below, diffracted.

In the distance, Mathilde recognised Pierre Dutour, Sylvie Jammet and Pascal Furion. They were smoking outside the building. When she reached them, they stopped talking.

That's how it began, with this silence.

This silence that lasts a few seconds, the embarrassed silence. They looked at each other. Sylvie Jammet began fishing for something in her bag. Eventually they acknowledged her with: 'Morning, Mathilde.' They pretended to continue their conversation but something stayed hanging in the air between them, between them and her. Mathilde went into the building, got out her card and swiped it in the time clock, which was showing 10.45. She waited for the beep and checked the screen: MATHILDE DEBORD: ENTRY REGISTERED. She went to the drinks machine and put some money in the slot.

She pressed the button and watched the cup fall and the liquid flow. She picked up the coffee and walked past the data-processing department. Jean-Marc and Dominique gave her a wave and she waved back. They didn't stop what they were doing. The glass door of Logistics was open. Laetitia was sitting at her desk, her phone glued to her ear. Mathilde felt as though she was avoiding her eye.

Something wasn't quite right, the usual ritual wasn't quite being observed.

It had spread, gone further.

Mathilde pressed the lift button and followed the lift's progress on the illuminated display.

Just as the doors opened, Laetitia came dashing out of her office and rushed in behind her. They kissed in greeting. Between the first and second floors, Laetitia stopped the lift. Her voice was shaking.

'Mathilde, he's replaced you.'

'What do you mean?'

'On Friday, when you weren't here, the girl from Communications, the one who was doing work experience, took your office.'

Mathilde was speechless. This didn't make any sense at all.

'They moved your stuff. They've put her in your place for good. Nadine told me they've given her a permanent job.'

'What job?'

'I don't know. That's all I was able to find out.'

Laetitia restarted the lift. Mathilde could hear the sound of her own breathing in the silence. There was nothing else to say.

Mathilde got out at the fourth floor. As the doors closed, she turned round and said, 'Thanks.'

Mathilde went along the corridor. She passed the open-plan area. They were all there: Nathalie, Jean, Éric and the others. Through the glass she could see them, absorbed, busy, in a state of great concentration. None of them looked up. She had become a shadow, impalpable, transparent. She no longer existed. The door to her office was open. Immediately she noticed that her Bonnard poster had disappeared. She could see a pale rectangle where it had been.

The girl was indeed there, sitting on *her* chair in front of *her* computer. Her jacket was hanging on *her* peg. She'd taken possession of the territory. Mathilde forced a smile. The girl answered her greeting in a weak voice without looking at her. She grabbed the phone and dialled Jacques's internal number.

'Mr Pelletier, Mathilde Debord is here.'

*

He came up behind her. He was wearing his black suit, the one for important days. He looked at the time on the clock and asked her if she'd had a problem. Everyone had been looking all over for her for two hours. Without waiting for her reply, he expressed concern about whether she was feeling better, if she'd had a rest, 'because you've been looking really tired lately, Mathilde'. Jacques glanced at the girl, watching her reaction. With just a few words hadn't he just given an outstanding demonstration of how good and kind he was? Just goes to show you shouldn't believe everything people say, the rumours that do the rounds . . . Mathilde began explaining that she had taken a day off to go on her son's school trip, but as she uttered the words she felt pathetic. Why did she have to justify herself? How had it come to this, providing justifications for her days off?

It was the first time he had spoken to her directly in weeks. In her high heels, she was a couple of inches taller than him.

A long time ago, on the way back from a meeting, Jacques had asked her if she could wear flat shoes, at least on days when they had to go out together. Mathilde had found this admission of weakness touching. They had laughed about it and she'd promised she would.

*

85

'As you can see, we've made some changes in your absence. I sent round a note last Friday explaining the objectives of this new structure, which will be achieved notably through a new organisation of space in order to facilitate the information flow within our team. In addition, we have the pleasure of welcoming Corinne Santos, who joined us this morning. Corinne has a similar background to you. She worked for a few months at L'Oréal in the international division and she's just finished a placement in Communications, where she worked wonders. She's going to help us set up the product plan for 2010, she . . .'

The sound of Jacques's voice faded out for a few minutes, was drowned out by a buzzing noise. Mathilde was standing facing him, but could no longer hear him. For a moment it seemed to her as though she was going to dissolve, disappear. For a few seconds all she could hear was a terrible deafening noise that came from nowhere. Jacques's eyes went from the girl to the window, from the window to the open door, from the open door back to the girl. Jacques was talking to her without looking at her.

'You'll find a copy of this note in your pigeonhole. In your absence, I took the liberty of having your things moved to 500–9, the empty office.'

*

Mathilde tried to get air into her lungs, air that would let her cry out or get angry.

There was no air.

'In order to avoid having to disconnect and reconnect all the equipment, Corinne will be using your computer from now on. Nathalie has copied your personal files on to a memory stick, which you can ask her for. IT will give you a new workstation as soon as possible. Any questions?'

The noise had stopped. There was a silence between them and she felt dizzy.

There were no words.

Corinne Santos looked at her. Corinne Santos's eyes said, 'I feel sorry for you. It's nothing to do with me. If it hadn't been me it would have been someone else.'

Corinne Santos's huge blue eyes were asking for forgiveness.

O n two occasions in January Mathilde asked for a meeting with the HR director. Patricia Lethu assumed a suitable expression and listened to her. She took notes and ticked boxes. She spoke to her in the affected way that people who are in good health adopt with those they have to handle carefully. Patricia Lethu explained patiently how complex the world of business had become, that it was subject to competitive pressures, to new markets opening up, not to mention EU directives, and how much all that, here as elsewhere, contributed to creating tension, stress and conflict. She described the harsh realities of business as though Mathilde were coming out of a convent or waking up from a long coma. With a sigh, Patricia Lethu added that HR directors all faced the same difficulties, it was a real headache, and in addition there was this ever-present pressure on objectives. It wasn't easy – it wasn't easy for anyone. You had to arm yourself, remain competitive, not allow yourself to be outpaced. Because it was undoubtedly true that those employees who were weakest psychologically would soon find themselves on the front line. Moreover, the business was doing a great deal of thinking about these issues and was considering setting up seminars run by outside consultants.

Patricia Lethu counselled patience. With time, things would get back to normal, a solution would be found. You had to accept that nothing was for ever, embrace change, make adjustments, be ready to reposition yourself. You had to take a good look at yourself. Maybe the time had come for Mathilde to think about a new direction, update her skills, take stock? Life sometimes forced us to take the initiative. Thus far Mathilde had been able to adapt. Patricia Lethu was confident that things would work out. She shook her hand.

Looking at it more closely, it's been noted in Mathilde's file that she is in a *conflict situation* with her superior. Over a sudden personality clash.

The company seeks information, takes note, considers the situation without investigating why it has come about, without examining whether the claim is well-founded. And by virtue of the same logic, it allows Mathilde to be deprived of her job. Because she's *incompatible*.

Given that confidence has been damaged, and bearing in mind the major challenges that marketing faces today, it is natural that Jacques should make arrangements and reorganise the department. Because the business must respond to constantly changing demands, give itself the ability to anticipate them, to win market share, to strengthen its international position, because the business cannot be content to follow, because the business must be cutting edge. That's what Patricia Lethu told her at their second meeting. As though she had learnt by heart the '2012 Horizon' leaflet put out by the head of PR.

Jacques's attitude, the reasons for his behaviour, the machinations Mathilde was subject to, cannot be considered in and of themselves. The scenario isn't foreseen in any software or on any checklist. The business agrees to recognise that there is a problem, which is the first step towards the search for a solution. Internal transfer seems most likely, but posts don't become available all that often, and some of them, when they do fall vacant, aren't being filled.

At the end of the meeting, in a more hushed tone (having made certain that the door was properly closed), in a sudden outburst of solidarity, Patricia Lethu advised her to put down in writing the points of disagreement with Jacques. And to send her emails with confirmation of receipt.

'But rest assured, we'll find a solution, Mathilde,' she hastened to add.

For a few weeks Mathilde no longer had anything to do. Nothing.

Not just a slack period, a slowing-down, a quiet stretch, a few days to catch her breath after a period of working flat out. Nothing as in zero, a complete void.

At the start, the team continued to seek her help, to consult her, to draw on her experience. But every document approved by her incurred Jacques's wrath. All it took was for her to have looked at a file, to have glanced at a study, or intervened in the choice of a contractor or a methodology, or given her agreement for a product plan, for him to oppose it. So gradually Nathalie, Jean, Éric and the others stopped coming into her office and asking her advice. They found the support they needed elsewhere.

They chose which side they were on.

So as not to risk being next on the list, to preserve their peace of mind. Through cowardice more than ill will.

She doesn't blame them. Sometimes she tells herself that at twenty-five or thirty, she wouldn't have had the courage either.

*

In any case, it's too late. Without realising it, she has allowed Jacques to construct a system of avoidance and exclusion, whose effectiveness is ever apparent and against which she can do nothing.

Her ring binders and files have been piled up, split between the shelves and the cupboard with sliding doors. Mathilde finds the contents of her drawer in a cardboard box on the floor: vitamin C, paracetamol, stapler, Sellotape, felt-tips, Tippex, biros and various supplies.

She's never had photos of her children on her desk. No vases, pot plants or holiday souvenirs. Apart from her Bonnard poster, she's brought nothing from home, hasn't tried to personalise her space or mark her territory.

She's always felt that the company was a neutral, emotion-free zone where those things didn't belong.

She's been transferred to office 500-9. She'll put away her things, settle in. She tries to persuade herself that it's not important, that it doesn't alter anything. She's above it. Should she feel attached to her office the way she would to a bedroom? That's ludicrous. Here at least she is far away from Jacques, far away from everything, at the other end.

At the end of the end, where no one comes except to go to the toilets.

Mathilde sits on her new seat, swivels, checks the castors. The desk and the side table are covered in a fine layer of dust. The metal filing cabinet doesn't match the rest. In fact, looking more closely, the furniture in room 500-9 is made up of disparate items that correspond to the firm's different periods: light wood, metal, white Formica. Room 500-9 has no window. The only source of light comes from the glazed panel which separates it from the supply store, which does have external light.

On the other side, room 500-9 shares a wall with the men's toilets for the floor, from which it is separated by a plywood wall.

In the company, room 500-9 is known as 'the storeroom' or else 'the shit-hole'. Because you can very clearly detect the smell of Glacier Freshness air freshener as well as the sound of the toilet-paper dispenser.

Legend has it that a restless trainee over the course of several weeks recorded precise statistics about the number of trips to the toilet and average consumption of toilet paper of all the managers on the floor. An Excel spreadsheet appeared on the desk of the managing director at the end of the study.

That's why room 500-9 stands empty most of the time.

*

Mathilde has placed the Argent Defender in front of her. She's more than half-tempted to talk to him, or rather murmur in a beseeching tone: 'So what are you going to do?'

The Argent Defender must have nodded off somewhere, taken a wrong turning in the corridor and ended up on the wrong floor. Like all princes and white knights, the Argent Defender displays a dubious sense of direction.

From where she sits with the door open, Mathilde can see all the comings and goings. Count, note, establish possible links. It's a distraction at least.

Éric has just gone by. He was looking straight ahead. He didn't stop.

Mathilde hears the sounds, identifying them one by one – the lock, the extractor fan, the jet of urine, paper, flush, washbasin.

She doesn't even want to cry.

She must have slipped by mistake into another reality. A reality she cannot understand or take in, a reality the truth of which she cannot grasp.

It's not possible. Not like this.

Without anything ever being said. Nothing that would allow her to go beyond, to make amends.

She could phone Patricia Lethu, ask her to come down right away and show her that she doesn't even have a computer any more.

She could throw her files around the room, fling them as hard as she can against the walls.

She could leave her new office, start shouting in the corridor, or sing Bowie at the top of her voice, play some chords on the air guitar, dance in the middle of the open-plan area, sway on her heels, roll on the ground so that people look at her, to prove that she exists.

She could call the managing director without going through his secretary, tell him she doesn't give a fuck any more about proactiveness, the optimisation of interpersonal skills, win-win strategies, the transfer of competence, and all these fuzzy concepts he's been feeding them for years, that he'd do better to get out of his office, to come and see what's going on, to smell the sickening stench that's invaded the corridors.

She could show up in Jacques's office armed with a baseball bat and methodically destroy everything: his collection of Chinese vases, the talismans he brought back from Japan, his 'director's' armchair in leather, his flat-screen and his CPU, his framed lithographs, the glass on his storage cabinet. She could tear down his Venetian blinds with her bare hands, with one gesture sweep all his marketing literature on to the floor and trample it in a fury.

*

Because there is this violence in her which surges up all at once: a continuous cry held back for too long.

This is not the first time.

The violence first appeared a few weeks ago when she realised what Jacques was capable of. When she understood that this had only just begun.

One Friday evening, when she had just got home, Mathilde received a call from Jacques's secretary. Jacques was held up in the Czech Republic. He had agreed to write an article for the in-house journal on product innovation in the division, but he was snowed under, he wouldn't have time. And so he'd asked Barbara to get in touch with Mathilde. The article had to be submitted by Monday morning at the latest.

For the first time in weeks, Jacques was asking something of her. Through an intermediary, it was true. But he was requesting her help. To do that, he must have uttered her first name, and recalled that she had written dozens of texts for him which he had signed without changing a single comma, or remembered at the very least that she was still part of his team.

The timing could have been better. Mathilde and the boys had planned to spend two days with friends. In addition, she was intending to take a half-day on Monday morning to go for an X-ray after the plaster came off her wrist.

She said yes. She'd cope somehow.

She took her laptop to the country and worked through most of the night from Saturday to Sunday. The rest of the time she laughed, played cards, helped prepare meals. She went walking by the river with the others, breathed in the smell of the earth in great lungfuls. And when people expressed concern about whether things at work had sorted themselves out, she said they had. Jacques's request was enough for her to believe that the situation could change, go back to how it was before, to believe that ultimately it was just a bad patch, a crisis they would get over and which she would forget in the end, because that was how she was – she didn't bear grudges.

On the Sunday night she sent the article to Jacques using the company's internal mail, which she could access remotely. He would have it when he got in on Monday morning, or perhaps even that evening if he was back. She fell asleep with a feeling of achievement she hadn't known in a long time.

The following day Mathilde took Théo and Maxime to school. Then she went to her appointment at the hospital, where she had to wait a good hour before she was seen. Later that morning she went back home, where she took advantage of the free moment to tidy the boys' cupboard and iron a few things. At one o'clock she bought a sandwich at the baker's down below and then she went to the metro station. The trains were almost empty and her journey seemed to flow smoothly. She dropped in at the Brasserie de la Gare for a coffee at the bar. Bernard complimented her on how well she was looking. At 2 p.m. on the dot she walked into the building.

Jacques was waiting for her. Scarcely had Mathilde got out of the lift when he began shouting.

'The article! What happened to the article?'

Mathilde felt the point of impact in her stomach.

'I sent it to you last night. Didn't you get it?'

'No, I didn't get anything. Not a thing. I waited all morning. I was looking for you everywhere and I had to cancel a lunch to write the bloody thing which I asked you to write on Friday night! I suppose you had better things to do than devote a few hours of your weekend to the company.'

'I sent it to you last night.'

'So you said.'

'I sent it, Jacques. If that weren't true, you know full well that I'd tell you.'

'Well, maybe it's time you worked out how your email system works.'

Faces appeared at half-open doors. There were furtive glances in the corridor. Stunned, Mathilde said nothing. Short of breath, she leaned against the wall. She had to retrace step by step what she had done after getting back on Sunday night, before she was able to visualise the scene: she had set the table, put the pizza in the oven and asked Simon to turn his music down. Then she switched on the laptop. Yes, she could see herself turning it on, sitting at the low table. Next she must have sent the article, nothing else was possible.

And then she began to have doubts. She was no longer sure. Perhaps she was interrupted and didn't send the email. Maybe she pressed a wrong key or got the wrong recipient or forgot the attachment. She wasn't sure about anything any more. Maybe she did forget to send the article. As simple as that.

The corridor was empty. Jacques had gone.

Mathilde rushed to her office, turned on her computer and entered her password. She waited for all the icons to appear and the anti-virus software to run. It felt like it was taking for ever. Her heart was in her mouth. At last she was able to open up her Sent box. There was the email on the first line, dated the night before at 19.45. She hadn't forgotten the attachment.

From her office she called Jacques to ask him to come and see for himself, to which he responded loud enough for everyone to hear: 'I didn't receive anything and I don't give a damn about salving your conscience.'

*

Jacques doubted her word.

Jacques spoke to her like a dog.

Jacques lied.

He *had* received her article. She knew that. He had probably used it as inspiration for his own.

Mathilde re-sent the email.

To prove to him that . . .

It was vain and ridiculous, a pitiful impulse to keep herself upright.

For the first time she imagined Jacques dead. His eyes upturned. For the first time she saw herself firing at point-blank range. She imagined the shot, powerful and irremediable. For the first time, she saw the hole in the middle of his forehead. Clean. And the burnt skin all around it.

Later, the image came back, and then came others: Jacques lying on the ground at the entrance to the building, a group of people gathered around his body, the trickle of white froth at the corner of his mouth.

Jacques in the blue light of the car park, dragging himself on his elbows, his legs broken, crushed, mangled, begging for forgiveness.

Jacques stabbed with his silver letter opener, pissing blood on his director's chair.

*

At the time, the images made her feel better.

Later, Mathilde felt afraid. That something was out of her control, was carrying her along, something she couldn't stop.

The images were so clear, so precise. Almost real.

Her own violence frightened her.

Thibault followed a case of gastro-enteritis on rue Bobillot with a panic attack on avenue Dorian and an earache on rue Sarrette.

At eleven o'clock he rang Rose to ask her if the controller was planning on having him shuttle between the two zones all day. He didn't want to be awkward, but Francis should try to minimise the number of trips, at least a bit, especially when they were only level-4 emergencies.

In fact Francis wasn't there. Francis was off sick. The base had had to call in a replacement controller. Rose went on: 'He's worked for SOS.'

Thibault was in a bad mood and couldn't hold back a comment. Maybe the replacement had fun making SOS doctors run all over Paris, but if she could explain to him that this wasn't their house style, he'd be really grateful.

Rose's voice trembled: 'Things are shit today, Thibault. I'm sorry. I might as well tell you right away that the direct line from the emergency services is ringing every three minutes. They're offloading tons of patients on to us. And you've got to go to rue Liancourt. There's a thirty-five-year-old man locked in his bathroom. He's having hallucinations and threatening to slit his wrists. He's already made four suicide attempts. His wife wants him hospitalised.'

That was all he needed. A 'mission'. In their slang that was the name they gave to the calls that no one wanted. Because in general they took up half the day. At the top of the list of 'missions' are instances of sectioning, arrests and death certificates.

Thibault said he was on his way. Because he's very fond of Rose and he is probably less worried than most about his hourly rate. He hung up.

A few seconds later he heard the beep of the text message giving him the entry code, floor and name of the person who called it in. He checked all the same that it wasn't a message from Lila. Just in case.

He knows what awaits him. If he doesn't manage to persuade the patient to sign a consent form voluntarily, he'll have to call the police, an ambulance and hope that it doesn't end like the last time. The girl managed to escape over the rooftops. And then she jumped. She wasn't even twenty.

That same evening, he remembers, he had arranged to see Lila. As soon as he was through the door, he wanted to throw himself into her arms, wanted her to gather him up, envelop him, wanted to feel the warmth of her body. To be free of himself for a few seconds. He made a movement towards her, a movement of abandon. And then in a fraction of a second, instinctively, the movement was cut short. Lila hadn't moved. Lila stood there in front of him, her arms by her sides.

He's been stuck for a good twenty minutes behind a van parked right in the middle of rue Mouton-Duvernet.

Two men are casually unloading clothes, sauntering, cigarettes in their hands. They disappear into a shop, then reappear several minutes later. They're in no hurry.

Thibault looks behind him. The traffic has built up; he can't reverse.

After the men's sixth return trip made with the same, vaguely ostentatious slowness, Thibault sounds his horn. Immediately the other cars do the same, as though they'd been waiting for his signal. One of the two men turns round towards him, his arm bent and his middle finger raised.

For a fraction of a second, Thibault imagines getting out of the car, rushing at the man and beating him up.

*

So he switches on the radio and turns up the volume. He breathes in.

Thibault has always been keen on changing sector when he requests his shifts. He has criss-crossed them all in every direction and in every fashion possible. He knows their rhythms and their geometry. He knows the squats and the townhouses, the houses covered in ivy, the names of the estates, the numbers on the stairwells, the ageing tower blocks and the brand-new apartment complexes which look like show homes.

For a long time he's believed that the city belongs to him. Because he knows its smallest street, tiniest alleyway, little-known mazes, the names of its new arterial roads, unlit passages, and the new developments by the Seine that have sprung up from nowhere.

He plunges his hands as far into the city's belly as possible. He knows the beating of its heart, its old aches which the damp reawakens, its moods and its pathology. He knows the colour of its bruises and the dizziness of its speed, its putrid secretions and its false modesty, its evenings of jubilation and the days after its celebrations.

He knows its princes and its beggars.

He lives above a square and never closes the curtains. He wants the light, the noise. The ceaseless circular movement.

He has long thought that he and the city beat to the same rhythm, are one and the same.

But today, after ten years behind the wheel of his white Clio, ten years of traffic jams, red lights, tunnels, one-way streets and double parking, it seems as though the city sometimes eludes him, that it has become hostile to him. It seems to him that because it is so over-crowded and because he recognises its fetid breath better than anyone, the city is waiting for its moment to vomit him up or spit him out, like a foreign body.

In her store cupboard, Mathilde checks that her phone line is working. She picks up the handset, dials zero and waits for the tone.

Reassured by the possibility of contact with the outside world, she hangs up.

She stretches on her chair, slides her palm over the Formica and listens for the sound of time silently passing. There are still two hours till lunch.

She would have liked to wear a skirt, to make her satin tights sparkle in the morning light. Because of her burn, she's had to put on trousers. Because it was the twentieth of May, she chose the lightest, most flowing ones.

Had she but known.

The phone rings and she jumps. Simon's mobile number appears on the screen, which confirms that her line has indeed been transferred.

His maths teacher is off and he wants to know if he can skip the canteen and go to his friend Hugo's for lunch and then back to school for the afternoon.

She says yes.

She'd like to talk to him, to prolong their exchange, win a few minutes from boredom, find out what life outside is like today, on the twentieth of May. She'd like to know if he has noticed something unusual in the air, a humidity, a languor, something which resists the city and its eagerness, which opposes it.

She can't ask him questions like that, as absurd as that – they'd scare him.

For a brief instant, she dreams that she could ask him to come home at once, to get his and his brothers' things ready, one bag each, no more. Because they're going away, right, now, all four of them. They're going away somewhere the air is breathable, where she can start all over again.

In the background she can hear street noise. He's going to his friend Hugo's for lunch. She can tell he's in a hurry. He's fourteen, he's got his life to live.

Mathilde sends him a kiss and hangs up.

She has her hands on either side of the phone. Her hands are like the rest of her body – inert.

Some way off, a photocopier is spitting out 150 sheets a minute. She listens to the machine's regular rhythm.

She tries to distinguish each note, each sound – the fan, the paper, the drive mechanism. She counts off – 112, 113, 114 . . . She remembers a winter's evening a long time ago when she had to stay late with Nathalie to finish a presentation on the department's activities. The office was empty. Before they left they had to print out four copies. Mathilde had pressed the green button and the repetitive, insistent noise of the machine had filled the whole place. And then the noise turned into music and they danced for as long as it lasted, barefoot on the carpet.

That was another time. A light, carefree time.

Today she has to pretend.

To look busy in an empty office.

To look busy without a computer or an Internet connection.

To look busy when everyone knows that she isn't doing anything.

When no one is waiting for her work any more, when her very presence is enough to make people look away.

Before, she used to check how her friends were getting on. She'd call them. A few stolen minutes when she got back after lunch or between two meetings later in the afternoon. She maintained the link, shared the day-to-day stuff. She'd talk about the children, her projects, where she'd been. Anecdotes and essentials. Now she doesn't call any more. She doesn't know what she'd say. She's got nothing to tell. She refuses dinner invitations, evenings out, she doesn't go to restaurants or the cinema any more. She doesn't leave the house any more. She's run out of excuses, she has got lost in ever vaguer justifications, has hidden herself from their questions, left their messages unanswered.

Because she can't go on pretending.

Because there always comes a moment when they ask: 'How're things at work?'

Under their scrutiny, she feels even more helpless. They probably say there's no smoke without fire, she must have done something wrong, slipped up. In their eyes, she's the one who's not doing so well. Who has problems. She's no longer one of them. She can't laugh about her boss any more, can't talk about her colleagues, feel pleased that the company's doing well, or worry about the difficulties it's having with that concerned look. The look of someone who works. She doesn't give a damn. She couldn't care less any more. They don't know the extent to which the little boxes they work in are hermetically sealed. The extent to which the air they breathe is polluted, saturated. Or else it's her.

Her who's not doing well. Who is no longer adapt-able. She who is too weak to get her way, mark her territory, defend her position. She whom the busi-ness has isolated for health reasons, like a tumour that's discovered late, a collection of unhealthy cells cut from the body. In their eyes, she feels judged. And so she keeps quiet. No longer answers. Crosses the street when she runs into them. Waves from afar.

And so for weeks she has been living in a closed circle with her children, expending energy for them that she no longer possesses. Nothing else matters.

And when her mother rings, she tells her she'll call back because she's snowed under.

The photocopier has stopped and silence has returned.

Oppressive.

Mathilde looks around. She wishes she could talk to someone. Someone who knows nothing about her situ-ation, who wouldn't feel sorry for her.

Because she has time, all the time in the world in fact, she decides to call the insurance company. She's been meaning to do it for several days to find out the amount she'll be able to claim on the orthodontic treat-ment that Théo is starting soon.

That's a good idea. That will occupy her.

Mathilde takes her insurance card out of her bag

and dials the number. The recorded message tells her that her call will be charged at thirty-four cents per minute. Excluding waiting time. The computerised voice asks her to press # and then choose the reason for her call by pressing 1, 2 or 3. The computerised voice suggests different scenarios among which she is supposed to recognise her situation.

To speak to someone – a real person with a real voice capable of giving a real answer – you have to break free of the menu. Not yield to the suggestions. Resist. Not press 1, 2 or 3. Maybe 0? To speak to someone, you have to be different, not fit any box, any category. You have to lay claim to your difference, not correspond to anything, to be quite simply *other*, in fact: with another reason, another request, another operation.

By doing this you sometimes manage to exchange a few words with a real person. Other times the recorded message loops back on itself, returning you to the main menu and it's impossible to get out.

The voice tells her that an adviser will respond in a few minutes. Mathilde smiles. She tries to identify the call-waiting music. She knows the tune, but that's all; she can't think what it is.

She waits.

At least she'll have spoken to someone.

*

She's put the phone on loudspeaker. With her head in her hands she has closed her eyes. She hasn't heard Patricia Lethu come quietly in. At the moment when their eyes meet, the music stops. The computerised voice announces that as all their advisers are currently busy, the company invites her to call back later.

Mathilde hangs up.

Patricia Lethu is blonde and tanned. She wears court shoes that match her suits and gold jewellery. She is one of those women who know that an outfit shouldn't combine more than three colours and that you should wear an odd number of rings. In summer she wears white, beige or oatmeal, reserving dark colours for winter. Every Friday she locks the door of her office and flies off to Corsica or somewhere, somewhere in the south, somewhere with nice weather.

She's said to be married to the number two in a big car manufacturer. She's said to have got her job with the company because her husband is the best friend of the president of the subsidiary. She's said to live in a vast apartment in the sixteenth arrondissement. She's said to have a lover who's younger than her, a senior manager in the holding company. Names do the rounds. Because, for several months,

Patricia Lethu has been wearing shorter and shorter skirts.

In the holidays Patricia Lethu goes to Mauritius or the Seychelles with her husband. She comes back more tanned than ever.

The HR director only leaves her office for special occasions – retirement parties, company meetings, Christmas celebrations. The rest of the time she has lots of work. You need to make an appointment.

This morning there's a bitter twist to her mouth. She looks around her with embarrassment.

Mathilde is silent. She has nothing to say.

The jet which a man releases when he urinates travels sufficiently far from his body to produce a splashing sound. Which covers the silence.

It's not long before they can hear the torrent of the flush. In the toilets someone coughs, then turns on the tap. Mathilde knows it's Pascal Furion because she saw him go in.

The smell of Glacier Freshness now pervades her office.

Patricia Lethu listens to the sounds coming from the other side of the partition. The blowing of the hand-dryer, another bout of coughing, the door closing. In normal circumstances Patricia Lethu is one of those women who know how to avoid silence. But not today. She doesn't even attempt a smile. Look at her closely and Patricia Lethu appears at a loss.

'I was told you had moved office. I . . . I didn't know. I wasn't here on Friday. I promise that . . . well . . . I've only just found out.'

'Me too.'

'I see that you don't have a computer. We'll sort that out. Think of this as a temporary solution. Don't worry, we'll—'

'You passed Jacques's office, didn't you?'

'Eh, yes.'

'Was he there?'

'Yes.'

'Did you speak to him?'

'No, I wanted to see you first.'

'Right, listen. I'm going to call him now. I'm going to call him in your presence and ask to speak to him. For the tenth time. Because I would like to know what to do, you see. Today, for example, in your opinion, what sort of work can I do without a computer, without having been to any team meetings and without having been copied in on any internal document for over a month? I am going to call him because Jacques Pelletier is my line manager. I'm going to tell him that you're here, that you've come down, and I'm going to ask him down too.'

Patricia Lethu gives a nod. She doesn't say a word. She must be finding it hard swallowing.

She has never seen Mathilde enraged like this. In a milder tone, Mathilde reassures her: 'Don't worry, Patricia. He won't answer. He never answers. But you'll see when you pass his office again that he's still there.'

Mathilde dials Jacques's number. Patricia Lethu holds her breath. She's rotating her wedding ring with her thumb.

Jacques doesn't pick up.

The HR director goes over to Mathilde and sits on the edge of her desk.

'Jacques Pelletier has complained that you've behaved aggressively towards him. He says it's become very difficult to communicate with you. That you show strong signs of resistance, that you're not on-message with the direction of the team, or of the company.'

Mathilde is stunned. She considers the phrase 'on-message' and how grotesque it seems. How far should she be *on-message* with, stick to, espouse, be at one with, melt into, merge with the company? Submit to it? She isn't *on message*. She'd like to know how being on message can be measured, how it can be counted, evaluated.

'Listen, it must be three months since I had a conversation worthy of the name with Jacques Pelletier and several weeks since he last spoke to me. Apart from this morning to tell me that my office had been moved. So I really don't see what this is about.'

'I ... well ... we shall resolve this problem. Of course, you are only here temporarily. I mean, this ... this can't go on.'

The rolling of the toilet-paper dispenser interrupts their exchange.

Suddenly it seems to her as though Patricia Lethu is going to collapse. Something in her eyes. Discouragement. Something which passes very quickly, an expression of disgust.

The HR director sweeps her hair back. She no longer dares look at Mathilde.

With a movement of her right foot, Mathilde sets her chair in motion. The castors glide her over to Patricia.

'I'm not going to hold it together, Patricia, I can't take any more. I want you to know. I've reached the limit of what I can bear. I've asked for explanations, I've tried to maintain a dialogue, I've been patient, I've done everything in my power to sort things out. But now, I warn you, I'm not going to . . .'

'I understand, Mathilde. This office, without light or a window . . . and so far away . . . I know . . . it's untenable.'

'You know as well as I do that it's not about the office. I want to work, Patricia. I take home three thousand euros a month and I want to work.'

'I'll . . . I'll take care of it. We'll find a solution. I'm going to start by calling IT so that they send someone as soon as possible to install a computer for you.'

Patricia Lethu has gone. As she went out the door, she turned back to Mathilde and repeated, 'I'll take care of it.' Her voice was tremulous, her blow-dry had lost some of its volume and movement. From behind she looked tired too.

'Our cause is to fight swiftly and mercilessly against any element of evil that surfaces in Azeroth.' For the moment he's dozing, resting, gathering his strength. Mathilde looks at the card. She wonders if Patricia Lethu saw it. She brings it closer, strokes it with her fingertips.

Then she looks beyond the card somewhere within her thoughts, which is none the less in front of her, a transparent space to which nothing sticks, on to which nothing can be projected.

The woman is wearing an old pair of jeans and a shapeless pullover whose sleeves hide her hands. The circles around her eyes are verging on violet. Her hair is unbrushed.

They are sitting in the living room. Thibault has asked her a series of questions about her husband's condition. He's on the other side of the door. They can hear him coughing. She told him that someone was coming. He called her a bitch and is now refusing to answer.

It began a few days earlier. He threw out the entire contents of the fridge on the grounds that it was poisoned, and kept checking over and over again that the gas was turned off. He refuses to turn on the light, or to sit or lie down. He spent the night standing in the hall. In the morning, after explaining to his wife that the forces of evil were infiltrating their home through the telephone cables and the ventilation ducts, he locked himself in the bathroom. He's been hospitalised several times before for severe bouts of depression, but until now he hasn't had delirious episodes. He's told her that he is going to do away with himself to protect her and the child. He wants her to leave the apartment, to go far away, as far away as possible, so that she's not contaminated by his blood. He's waiting for her to go.

The woman moves her chair.

That's when Thibault discovers a little girl behind her. He hadn't seen her come in. A tiny silhouette, nestling against her mother, staring at him, her eyes wide with fear.

In ten years of medical emergencies, he's seen his fair share of anguish, distress and madness in close-up. He knows suffering, its accents of terror; he knows how it floods in, how things go awry and get lost. He knows the violence of it, he has grown accustomed to it.

But not to this.

The child is watching him. She can't even be six.

'Aren't you at school?'

She shakes her head and hides behind her mother again.

'I couldn't take her. I didn't want my husband to be left alone.'

Thibault gets up and goes over to the girl. She looks at his left hand. He smiles. Children are always quicker to notice his disability.

'I'd like you to go and play in your room for a bit because I have things to say to your mother.'

Thibault explained to the woman that he would try to persuade her husband to be hospitalised. But if he failed, he'd have to call the police and get her to sign the request for committal herself. Because her husband presented a danger to himself and perhaps also to his family.

He went over to the door and crouched down so that he was at the same level as the man whose breathing he could hear. He talked to him for half an hour. In the end the man opened the door and Thibault went into the bathroom. The man was calm. He let Thibault listen to his chest. He took his pulse. He told the man that his blood pressure was much too high, a trick he often uses to convince a patient that hospitalisation is necessary. The man agreed to an injection. They talked for another ten minutes and then he gave in.

Even in the depths of delirium, even in the most acute manic episodes, there is a crack. A tiny chink of lucidity through which you have to intervene.

The ambulance arrived. Thibault stayed with the man until he got into the vehicle. Once the doors had closed, he instinctively looked up. Behind the glass the little girl was watching him.

What will she remember of these images, of this time in suspension, of these days when things slid out of control?

What kind of adult do you become if you have discovered at such an early age that life can collapse? What kind of person? What does it equip you with? What are you missing?

The questions returned as they did every time. The questions come when it's all over. When he's finished work and left behind people who've been destroyed whom he'll never see again.

Thibault got back in his car. Lila's perfume hung in the air, an invisible trace which tore at his throat.

He turned his mobile back on. Two new addresses were waiting for him. The first of them wasn't too far. He turned the key in the ignition. He was assailed at once by her absence. In compact form.

As soon as he's in the car, her absence presents its challenge.

At a red light, he's thinking of her. When his foot presses on the accelerator, he's thinking of her. When he changes gear, he's thinking of her.

It's half past twelve and he isn't hungry. There's a hole where his stomach was. A rough pain. Something oppressive, burning, which doesn't call for any food or any comfort.

He met Lila one autumn night in the Bar des Oies, in that part of the street that climbs towards the sky. Before then, they had bumped into each other several times near where he lived, outside the swimming pool or near the baker's. This time they were so close it was impossible to miss each other. Leaning on the bar, he looked at the bracelet on her wrist, which didn't go with the rest of her outfit, it contradicted it. And then her thin legs and her too high heels, and such fine ankles that he wanted to hold them between his fingers. He had just finished a twelve-hour shift. She had come up to him or the other way round; he couldn't say, he doesn't remember. She wasn't like the women he went for, but they had several drinks and then their tongues met. On the bar Lila had caught hold of his left hand and stroked his scar with the tips of her fingers. There was chemistry between them – foreign bodies sometimes mix, go well together, merge. Between them it had been a physical thing without any doubt. And as he hadn't entirely given up on his childhood experiments, he had wanted to see if this mixing of skins was capable of transformation, and of completion.

If the chemistry – by contagion or diffraction – could spread and turn to passion.

But very soon he had collided with her. *Collided* – that was the word. Very soon he collided with her reserve, her distance, her moments of absence. Very soon he understood that she could only love him when horizontal, or when he held her on top of him by her hips. Afterwards, he would watch her sleep on the other side of the bed, remote. From the start, he had collided with the air of indifference with which she countered anything that smacked of emotion, with her closed expression the morning after, her gloomy moods at the end of the weekend, her inability to manage the simplest goodbye.

Even after the most intense nights, in the morning she offered him this closed face, on tiptoe, without any sign of emotion. Never when they were on the point of parting did he dare to hold her to him. Likewise, when they saw each other again after a gap of several days or weeks, the impulse which always propelled him towards her seemed to offend her, to jolt her immobility. He could get no purchase. Nothing to latch on to.

She didn't open her arms.

He had long wondered if Lila was like that because that was her nature, if this refusal to be demonstrative outside the bed was just the way she was, a given which he had to accept and about which he could do nothing.

Or if conversely it was reserved for him, affected only him, a silent reminder of the way they were developing, and that all they were playing out was a physical affair, not something which from any vantage point could resemble a relationship. They weren't *together*. They didn't constitute anything – they had no geometry, no shape. They had met and been happy to repeat that encounter each time they saw each other – to mix one with the other and notice the fact of that fusion.

Lila was his downfall. His punishment for all the women he'd been incapable of loving, the ones he'd seen for just a few nights, the ones he'd ended up leaving – because something he couldn't name kept coming back. It was ridiculous, but he had thought: the time had come for him to settle the account.

A love affair perhaps simply came down to this imbalance: as soon as you wanted something, expected something, you'd lost.

Chemistry could do nothing in the face of Lila's memory and her unresolved past loves. He was utterly weightless compared to the man she was waiting for, hoping for, a smooth man who was unlike him.

And words, like liquids, had evaporated.

On rue Daviel he's parked on a pedestrian crossing.

He doesn't want to circle the block three times looking for a space. He's tired.

Passers-by give him filthy looks. It doesn't matter that he has a sign and a badge on the side of his car, he's on their turf. In the city, you're either a pedestrian, a cyclist or a driver. You walk, pedal or drive. You look people over, size them up, and despise them. In the city, you have to decide which side you're on.

A little further on, Mrs L.'s waiting for him. Her baby has a fever of 102. He knows her. He sees her four times a month. She weighs, measures, watches, checks. She manufactures worry. The base is unable to refuse to send out a doctor. A matter of responsibility. Nine times out of ten, it's Thibault who goes. Because Mrs L. knows him and he doesn't lose patience with her. And in addition, she asks for him.

He has to pick up his bag, get out of the car and close the door.

This time he's the loser. He loves a woman who doesn't love him. Maybe there's nothing more violent than the acknowledgement of this powerlessness? Maybe there's no worse sorrow, worse malady?

No, he knows that's not so. That's ridiculous. It's untrue.

Unrequited love is no more nor less than a kidney stone. The size of a grain of sand, a pea, a marble or a golf ball – a crystallised chemical substance likely to cause a sharp, indeed unbearable, pain. But which always goes in the end.

He hasn't undone his seat belt. From behind his windscreen he looks at the city. Its never-ending ballet in spring colours. An empty plastic bag which dances in the gutter. A man bent over at the post-office entrance whom no one seems to notice. Green dustbins overturned on the pavement. Men and women going into a bank, passing each other on a crossing.

He watches the city, all these superimposed actions. This place of endless intersections where people never meet.

Mathilde has put her files on the shelves, her pens in a pot and arranged her supplies of stationery in her drawer. That has taken her the best part of an hour, by making sure she moved slowly, that each decision came after several minutes of deliberation, to put things here or there, at the edge or in the middle, above or below, destined for this or that use.

Once again she's waiting.

Someone knocks at the door. Two technicians from IT are standing there, waiting for her to tell them to come in. She indicates that they should. She knows them. They look after the computer network for the whole site. She often passes the tall one in the corridor. The small one she sees when she has lunch in the cafeteria. He has a loud laugh, you can't miss him.

Mathilde stands up and moves aside to make room.

They exchange pleasantries about the weather. She goes along with it, expressing pleasure on hearing that the next few days will be fine. As if that mattered. As if that could have any impact on the train of events. And then they set to work. They unpack, unroll, connect, assemble.

In no time at all they've installed a new computer. The tall one goes through the final steps to configure the machine.

Meanwhile the small one contemplates Mathilde's cleavage as she sits there. She's wearing one of those push-up bras that make your breasts look bigger. The lacey straps are the same colour as her blouse. She has never given up on her appearance. She dresses as she used to. Wears a skirt, a suit, puts on make-up. Even if sometimes she doesn't have the energy. Even if coming in pyjamas or a tracksuit would probably make no difference.

There. The tall one starts up the computer, goes over to Mathilde and explains. By default she is linked to the printer on that floor, laser Infotec XVGH3018. If she wants to print in colour, she needs to select another printer.

Mathilde tries to work out how long it's been since she's had to print a document.

The tall one sees the card lying near her.

'The Argent Defender! You're lucky! My son would sell both his parents for that card. Is it yours?'

'Yes, my son had a dupe and gave it to me.'

'I'll buy it off you!'

'Oh no, I couldn't . . .'

'Come on. I'll give you ten euros.'

'I'm sorry, I can't.'

'Twenty?'

'I'm really sorry. It was a gift. And anyway . . . I really need it.'

They say goodbye and go off.

She hears them laughing in the corridor.

She said she really needed it. As though her life depended on it.

Mathilde picks up the mouse and goes over to the keyboard. She clicks on Internet Explorer. The Google page comes up and she types 'World of Warcraft'.

She has no difficulty in finding the rules. WoW was a video game and an online game before it became a card game. It has thousands of followers around the world.

She reads attentively.

On the other side of the Dark Portal, every player is a hero. The cards he holds allow him to equip himself with arms and armour, to use spells and talents, and to recruit allies to his group. In the course of the game, the cards allow you to inflict damage on opposing heroes or to protect against their attacks. The aim of the game is to kill your enemies. Each hero has a health value printed in the lower right corner, which tells you how much damage the hero can take. If your hero takes damage greater than or equal to his health ('fatal damage'), you're out of the game. Your hero can attack and defend against opposing characters, but to deal damage in combat, your hero must usually strike with a weapon. Dead cards – destroyed or discarded ones – go to a player's cemetery.

In the cemetery, cards must be placed face down.

Mathilde looks at the Argent Defender.

His health value is 2,000 points.

As he is a defender, he can't be used for attack.

The problem is that Mathilde has only one card.

The problem is that she has already suffered a certain amount of damage.

And she doesn't know how many points she has left.

In the past, she used to have lunch with Éric, Jean or Nathalie. Sometimes they'd all have lunch together – the whole team.

Now they disperse – some go to the canteen, others to the restaurant. They don't tell her.

Her allies have disappeared, they have taken the side roads. They are stealing out of Azeroth. They have 'lunches out', shopping to do. They grab a quick sandwich.

From time to time, Éric or Nathalie suggests going out with them. When Jacques is overseas. When they know he's far away.

It's one o'clock. The office has emptied all at once, like a school class when the bell goes.

For several weeks, Mathilde has generally had lunch with Laetitia, in the canteen or elsewhere. Laetitia works in Logistics. They met on an in-house course and they've kept in touch.

But this lunchtime Laetitia can't make it. She has a dentist's appointment; she's sorry. If she had known . . . Today of all days, it's such bad timing. Briefly, Mathilde tells her about Patricia Lethu's impromptu visit. At the other end of the line, Laetitia gives a grim laugh.

'It's time they faced up to the problem, Mathilde. I can well understand that she's caught between two stools, but hey, that's part of her job. A sort of contradiction in terms if you see what I mean. She's got to choose. Take responsibility. Because the time is coming when she won't be able to look after the fox and the goose.'

'The fox ate the goose a long time ago.'

'That's what you think, and that's the problem. But you're still there, Mathilde. You've held on for eight months in a situation where other people would have been destroyed. You're holding on, Mathilde, but it's time this stopped.'

Laetitia has a simple vision of the company. It's quite similar to the one that rules Azeroth. The good fight to assert their rights. The good are not without ambition but refuse to cause devastation and use mean tricks to attain their ends. The good have ethics. They don't trample on their neighbours. The evil have invested their lives in the quagmire of the company, and the only identity they have is the one written on their payslip. They are ready to do anything to climb the ladder or move up a grade. They long ago renounced their principles, if by chance they ever had any.

Laetitia's speeches, her no-nonsense language, her way of dividing the world in two, used to make Mathilde smile. Sometimes they disagreed. Now she wonders if Laetitia hasn't been right all along. If business isn't the ultimate testing ground for morality. If business isn't by definition a place of destruction. If business with its rituals, its hierarchy, its ways of functioning, is not quite simply the sovereign place of violence and impunity.

Every day Laetitia comes to work armed with the same jovial humour. She has drawn a clear line between her private and professional lives. They don't mix. She's impervious to the malicious gossip and office rumours, she couldn't care less if Patricia Lethu is Pierre Chemin's mistress or whether Thomas Fremont is homosexual. She walks the corridors, chin up, with a haughty air she's made her own. She breathes different air, that's purer and more refined. She clocks out at six thirty every evening. Her life is elsewhere.

Laetitia was the first to guess what was happening to Mathilde. Little by little. She caught snatches of conversations. Here and there. She realised what was going on even before Mathilde. She has never stopped asking her questions, insisting on details, hasn't been fobbed off with evasive replies or lines that trail away. She has respected her silence, her sense of shame. But she has never let it drop.

The phone rang again. It was Patricia Lethu. The HR director wanted to let her know that she had things in hand. She's sent her CV to all the subsidiaries in the group and picked out some internal job ads that might interest her. She's seeing Jacques in the afternoon to raise some questions with him. Things will work themselves out. Just as Mathilde was about to hang up, Patricia Lethu stopped her. Her voice has recovered a sort of reassurance.

'I perhaps didn't appreciate your difficulties soon enough, Mathilde, and I'm sorry about that. But I want you to know that I am attending to it. I'm making it my personal business.'

It's 1.20. Mathilde's still waiting to try to go out. She doesn't want to bump into Jacques or anyone else from her floor. She puts on her jacket, slips the Argent Defender into her bag and heads for the lift.

The door to Jacques's office is shut.

*

As Mathilde leaves the building, she hesitates to go to the company restaurant. From where she is, she can see the queue running a few yards along the outside of the building.

Finally she goes over and takes her place in it. She'll eat lunch quickly and then go to Bernard's for a coffee. She checks she hasn't forgotten her swipe card for the self-service.

She waits behind the others, looking at her feet. Her turn comes and she slips through the door. Once she's inside, she has a few more minutes to wait till she gets to the food.

You have to take a tray, slide it along the rails, and choose between the weightwatcher's menu, the gastronomic menu and the exotic menu. Choose between beetroot decorated with a thin slice of lemon, grated carrots with egg mayonnaise on top, or celeriac salad and parsley flowers. You pick up a bread roll with tongs, one or two sachets of salt and wait for the cashier. You give them your card and take your receipt. Say hello, bon appétit, thanks, wave, smiles fading. You choose a table, eat amid the hubbub of office conversations, unchanging, gone bad.

Mathilde has sat down by herself behind a pillar. She keeps her eyes fixed on her plate, swallowing mechanically. She allows herself to drift off into the noise, and then the words come back: the world keeps turning like the hem of a flowery dress, Jacques Pelletier says that, I didn't know, I'm going to take care of it, you show signs of resistance, the train for Melun will arrive at platform 3, I'm going to take care of it, cards allow you to recruit allies to your group, you're not on-message with the direction of the business, you're only here temporarily, because there comes a point when you can't look after the fox and the goose any more, I didn't appreciate your difficulties soon enough, I'm going to start by calling IT, this can't go on, the damage done is permanent and irreversible. The damage done is permanent and irreversible.

Mathilde got up without finishing her lunch, put her tray on the trolley and left. She walked to the Brasserie de la Gare and sat down at a small table in the middle. Bernard came out from behind the counter to greet her.

He's sitting opposite her, smiling.

He can tell that she has lost points, several hundred, since this morning.

She'd like him to take her in his arms. Just like that, without a word, only for a moment. To rest for a few seconds, to get support. To feel her body relax. Breathe in the smell of a man.

At work, they say that the café owner is in love with her. That he asked her to marry him. They say that every morning he waits for the moment when Mathilde comes in for her coffee. That he's hoping that one day she'll change her mind.

Bernard has gone back behind the counter and is rinsing glasses.

Sometimes she dreams of a man she could ask: could you love me? With all her tired life behind her, its strength and its fragility. A man who would have known dizziness, fear and joy. Who wouldn't be afraid of the tears behind her smile, nor of her laughter amid the tears. A man who would understand.

But desperate people don't meet. Or maybe only in films. In real life, their paths cross, they brush shoulders, perhaps collide. And often they repel each other like the identical poles of two magnets. She's known that a long time.

Now Mathilde is watching a girl and a boy at the back of the café, their legs intertwined under the table. They are young. The girl's wearing a really short skirt and is talking loudly. The boy's eyes are devouring her. They are sharing a plate of spaghetti. The boy's hand is stroking the girl's thigh.

*

Mathilde's waiting for her coffee. She's thinking about the question that Simon asked her the other day point-blank: 'How do you know you're a couple?'

She was preparing dinner and he'd sat down near her to do his homework. The twins were in their room.

She knew that he had been going out with a girl for a while, that he was in love.

She tried to find an answer, a proper one, for a long time.

She said, 'Wait, I'm thinking.' Then, a few seconds later: 'When you think about the other person every day, when you need to hear their voice, when you worry about whether they're all right.'

Simon was looking at her. This wasn't enough. He was waiting for something more.

'When you're able to love the other person just as they are, when you're the only one who can see what they are capable of becoming, when you want to share what's essential, and to project it onto a new surface which you've invented . . . I don't know. When it has become more important than every-thing else.'

She wished there could have been two of them to answer these questions.

That *she* was still part of a couple, in fact.

She's alone and she replies with just one voice. A voice that's diminished and stunted. Her sons are growing up and they lack a father. His male perspective, his way of looking at the world, his experience.

She's a woman faced with three boys who will continue to grow up, change, transform. She's alone, faced with their strangeness.

Philippe died ten years ago.

Ten years.

Philippe's death is part of her. It's inscribed in every cell of her body. In the memory of fluids, bones and stomach. In the memory of her senses. And that first day of spring, bathed in sunlight. A pale scar that blends in with her skin.

For the first time since the birth of the twins they were going away for the weekend without the children. Just the two of them. Théo and Maxime had just turned one. It had been a year of broken nights, sleepwalking, vegetable purées and bottles at the right temperature. A year of machines to fill, washing to hang out, overflowing shopping trolleys pushed up and down the aisles of Carrefour.

They had just left the three boys with Philippe's parents at their house in Normandy and were driving towards the sea. They felt exhausted. Mathilde had booked them in to a hotel in Honfleur. Philippe was driving. She watched the trees by the roadside go by and then she fell asleep.

And then there was a high-pitched noise, the screeching of tyres on tarmac, like a shriek. The numbness of sleep ripped apart. When Mathilde opened her eyes, they were in the middle of a field, down below the level of the road. The front of the car was smashed in and Philippe's legs were beneath it. All the lower part of his body below his waist had been swallowed up in the metal.

Philippe was conscious. He wasn't in pain.

The car had rolled over ten or twelve times before hitting a tree. She found that out later.

She looked around at the trees, the fields as far as the eye could see. Her body had begun to shake, she could no longer breathe. Silently, the terror was swelling.

They were no longer driving to the hotel. They weren't going to have dinner in a restaurant or spend hours caressing each other between the sheets. They wouldn't linger in bed. They wouldn't take baths and drink wine late into the night.

They were there, side by side in the middle of nowhere. Something serious had happened. Something irremediable.

She stroked his face and neck. She brushed her fingers over his mouth. His lips were dry. He smiled.

Philippe asked her to go and get help. No one could see them from the road.

Mathilde's knees were knocking together. So were her teeth.

Her door was jammed. She had to force it. She got out of the car, walked round it and went over to his side. She looked through the window, saw his legs and his hips swallowed up and hesitated for a moment. Everything seemed so calm.

She turned around one last time and then she went off. Then the sobs came, tearing at her throat. She walked to the slope. She grabbed hold of bushes and tall grass to pull herself up. Her palms were cut until they bled. She stood on the verge and raised her arms. The first car that came along stopped.

When she went back down, Philippe had lost consciousness.

He died three days later.

Mathilde had just turned thirty.

She has few memories of the months that followed. It was an anaesthetised, amputated period that no longer belongs to her. It lies beyond her, hidden from memory.

*

After the funeral she and the boys moved in with her parents. She swallowed white and blue pills, arranged by dose in a transparent box. She stayed in bed for days at a time, staring at the ceiling. Or stood in her childhood bedroom with her back to the wall, unable to sit down. She spent hours curled up under the scalding shower until her mother came and helped her up.

At night she felt her way around in silence, opening the door to watch the boys sleeping. Or else she'd lie down on the floor by their beds. She'd let her hand rest on their bodies, bring her face close to their mouths until she could feel them breathing.

She was drawing strength from them.

It seemed to her then that she could spend the rest of her life there. Looked after. Sheltered from the world. With nothing to do but listen to the throb of her sorrow. And then one day she felt afraid. Of becoming a child again. Of never being able to leave.

And so little by little she relearned. Everything. To eat, to sleep, to look after the boys. She came back from a bottomless torpor, from the depths of time.

At the end of the summer she went back to the flat. She tidied, sorted, emptied. She gave Philippe's things to charity. She kept his records, his silver ring and his Moleskine notebooks. She found a new place to live.

She moved. Simon started school. She began to look for work.

A few months later, she met Jacques for the first time. After three meetings, he hired her. Her mother came every day to look after Théo and Maxime until Mathilde got them places in a nursery.

She had started work again. She took the RIVA train, she spoke to people, every morning she went somewhere where she was expected, she belonged to a team, she gave her opinion, talked about the rain or the nice weather at the coffee machine.

She was alive.

She and Philippe had been happy. They had been in love. She had been lucky that way. Those years were written on her body. Philippe's laugh, his hands, his genitals, his eyes burning with exhaustion, the way he danced, walked, took the boys in his arms.

Today Philippe's death doesn't hurt any more.

Philippe's death is an absence which she has tamed. Which she has learned to live with.

Philippe is the missing part of her, an amputated limb of which she has retained a precise sensation.

Today Philippe's death no longer impedes her breathing.

*

At the age of thirty, she survived the death of her husband.

Now she is forty, and a stupid bastard in a three-piece suit is in the process of destroying her slowly, by degrees.

Mathilde drank her coffee and left the money on the table. Outside, she raised her face to the sky and remained like that for a moment, watching the clouds scudding by, swift and silent.

For a few seconds she thought about going to the station, not returning to the office. Going home, drawing the curtains and lying down on the bed.

She hesitated. She felt as though her body no longer had the strength.

However, she took the same route as that morning. She walked to the office and slipped through the revolving door. As she got another coffee from the machine, she thought that she was drinking too much of the stuff. She took the lift and walked past the large windows. In the distance she could hear Jacques's voice, but she didn't look. She walked along the corridor to her new office. She took off her jacket and sat down. She shook the mouse to wake the computer.

While she was out, someone had left the memory stick with her personal files on her desk.

*

She's just a brave little soldier. Used up, limping, ridiculous.

She hasn't wanted to let go. To give ground. She has wanted to be here, keeping her eyes open. From an absurd display of pride or courage, she has wanted to fight. Alone.

Now she knows that she was wrong.

On a new notepad, she makes a list of things she could do to pass the time. Phone the train company and book tickets for the holidays, explore the World of Warcraft site and expand her knowledge of the rules of the game, do some online shopping at La Redoute, send an email to the managing agent about the bike park for which no one has a key.

She's got to make it to six o'clock.

Even if she has nothing to do. Even if it's pointless.

Mathilde takes the Argent Defender out of her pocket and places it just in front of her.

When the computer goes into standby mode, the screen turns into an aquarium. Fish of all colours bump against the glass, and go from one side to the other endlessly.

They swim past each other, rub against each other. Fine bubbles come from their mouths. They don't seem to suffer.

Maybe the answer is there, in their unconsciousness.

So life in a bowl is possible as long as everything slides along, as long as nothing collides and no one panics.

And then one day the water turns cloudy. At first it's imperceptible. The merest haze. Some particles of silt settle at the bottom, invisible to the naked eye. But silently, something is decomposing. You don't exactly know what. And then the oxygen begins to run out.

Until the day when one of the fish goes mad and starts to devour all the rest.

When Thibault got back to his car, there was a ticket fluttering on the windscreen. He went into the nearest café. The noise assailed him immediately. For a moment he almost turned back. After ordering a sandwich at the counter, he sent a text to Rose to let her know that he was taking a twenty-minute break.

Thibault sits down on a vacant stool. He's turned off his mobile.

He's tired. He would like a woman to take him in his arms. Without saying anything, just for a moment. To rest for a few seconds, to gain support. To feel his body relax. Sometimes he dreams about a woman who he'll ask: 'Could you love me?' With all his tired life behind him. A woman who would have known dizziness, fear and joy.

Could he love another woman?

Now.

Could he desire another woman? Her voice, her skin, her perfume. Would he be ready to start over, once again? The game of meeting, the game of seduction, the first words, the first physical contact, first mouths and then genitals. Does he still have the strength?

Or has something been amputated? Is there now something he lacks, something missing?

Start over. Once again.

Is it possible? Does it have any meaning?

Beside him a man in a dark suit is eating his lunch standing up and leafing through a newspaper. He would like to close his eyes, not to hear anything any more, to absent himself for as long as it takes for something within him to grow calm, something which he cannot contain.

'Do I know what it means to be with someone? What form that can take, at my age, what it's like, with all the pathetic little love affairs that you drag behind you. Do you know?'

Thibault turned towards a woman sitting on his other side. For a moment he thought she was talking to herself, and then he saw the earpiece in her ear and the microphone dancing in front of her mouth. She's speaking louder and louder, indifferent to people looking at her.

'No, I don't believe it any more. You're right, yes, that's it exactly! I don't believe in it any more. I don't want to be taken for a ride. Because I'm heartsick. Yes,

I'm scared. Yes, if you like. So? Fear is sometimes a good counsellor. I . . . what?'

She's sitting with her legs crossed, her back straight, perched as if by some miracle atop her stool, one heel resting on the steel bar. Her mobile is lying in front of her. She's looking at her empty glass, absolutely unaware of what's around her, waving her arms about as she talks.

He would like to put his right hand on this woman's shoulder to attract her attention. To say, could you just shut up? All we can hear is you.

Behind him a dozen conversations mingle with the sounds of cutlery and chairs scraping on the floor. Behind him people are drinking, laughing, complaining.

He wants to be alone. He feels hot and cold at the same time. He's not sure if he's getting a migraine but thinks he may be. He's aware of his body in a strange way. His body is a wasteland, abandoned ground, yet linked to all this disorder. His body is under pressure, ready to implode. The city is suffocating, pressing down on him. He is tired of its randomness, its shamelessness, its fake intimacies. He is tired of its feigned moods and the illusion that men and women ever really connect. The city is a deafening lie.

'So what do you think of it?'

Laetitia has burst into her office without knocking. She twirls around, poses, moves back and forth, waiting for Mathilde's verdict.

'It's fantastic. It really suits you. Did you get it at the weekend?'

'Yes. It's completely crazy since I've already got it in blue and black . . . You know, the one I was wearing the other day . . . It's the same . . . When I got home I felt pathetic.'

'You shouldn't! Just tell yourself that your buying policy follows an implacable logic. That there's coherence in the way you approach clothes, a sort of consistency.'

Laetitia laughs.

Mathilde really likes this girl. Her way of diverting her, not starting with a drama, avoiding compassion.

Laetitia hasn't come in with the overwhelmed look that anyone else would have adopted in the circumstances. She's come in with her new jacket and this apparent triviality which she has never given up.

'And what about you? Have you made up your mind about seeing Paul Vernon? Because you need to have the union behind you now, Mathilde. You won't manage it on your own. You're not up to it. That guy is sick, and he's not finished giving you a hard time. You were his creature, his thing, and then you escaped him. That's what people are saying, you know. Among other things. It won't sort itself out by itself, Mathilde.'

Laetitia looks around.

'But seriously, look at this, it's shameful!'

Laetitia doesn't lower her voice. She wants people to hear her. Any louder and she'd be standing in the corridor with a megaphone crying scandal.

'Patricia Lethu called me back a little while ago. She's taken things in hand. She's really trying to find me something else. I believe that she's taking care of it.'

'Listen, Mathilde, that's all well and good. But for your part you mustn't let anything go. You must protect yourself. Continue exactly as if the war was going to go on. You must anticipate the worst.'

And then after a silence, Laetitia adds: 'Watch out. Promise me you'll see Paul, even if just for advice. You need to get help, Mathilde. You can't do it on your own.'

*

Laetitia has gone. She has a meeting.

Mathilde didn't manage to tell her that she called Paul Vernon. Last week. Within a few moments, Paul Vernon got the picture. He repeated to her several times that she must not resign. Whatever happens, on no account. He explained to her how to keep records of everything, to note every detail, to describe in the most factual manner possible what has changed, the objective development of the situation. He suggested that she write down a sort of chronology that traced the deterioration in her relationship with Jacques stage by stage, noting the key dates. She must compile a dossier.

Nothing in Mathilde's account seems to surprise him. Neither the situation in which she found herself, nor the time it had taken her to call.

He said, 'In cases like this, people always wait too long. They try to fight and they run out of steam.'

If things turn nasty, you need witnesses. She'll need proof that she was taken off projects, that the content of her job was changed. She needs to bring proof that she no longer has objectives, that she has been marginalised. Other people need to stick their necks out and support her. Her colleagues. People in her team. People in other teams. Because nothing of course is written down or official. Nothing is verifiable.

Paul Vernon had to go to an industrial tribunal about a sacking on a production site. Mathilde promised to call him back.

That was a week ago and she hasn't done it. In spite of all the empty time before her, she hasn't begun writing the document he asked for either.

She didn't tell Laetitia that she called Paul Vernon because she no longer has the strength. Because it's too late. She isn't up to doing what he needs her to. She can't talk any more, she's got no more words. She who used to be feared for her rhetorical flair. She who was able to get her point of view acknowledged, alone against ten, when she stood in for Jacques at the management committee. On the phone Paul Vernon didn't realise it, but it's too late. Now she is one of the weak ones, in the sense that Patricia Lethu means it. The transparent, shrivelled, silent people. Now she is fading away in an office by the loos because it's the only place she deserves. There is no reason for this to stop.

Mathilde looks at the list she's just written, those tiny things that she can't manage.

Éric passes her office to go to the toilet and glances furtively in but doesn't stop.

She hears him on the other side of the partition: lock, ventilator, stream of urine, paper, flush, washbasin.

He passes her door again and Mathilde calls to him.

He comes in hesitantly, ill at ease, and she says, 'Sit down.'

Over the past few weeks, Mathilde has developed a sort of intuition about the position of other people as allies or adversaries. In the world of Azeroth, on the threshold of the Dark Portal, it's important to recognise who's on your side.

She recruited Éric herself three or four years ago. She fought to get him appointed. He's become one of the best product chiefs on the team.

But Éric eludes her recognition system. He's a blur.

'Éric, I'd like to ask you something.'

'Yes?'

'Could you write a letter with some precise, concrete facts. Not a letter against Jacques or against anyone, more like an account of the current situation. For example, that I don't have direct responsibility for the team any more, I don't run the planning meeting and that I'm not involved in any decisions. Just that. To record that I don't take part in anything any more.'

There was a silence. Éric's cheeks turned a deep red.

He looked around, the windowless office, the dusty furniture. He rubbed his hands mechanically on his thighs and moved his chair back. He spoke without looking at her.

'I can't, Mathilde. You know that I can't risk losing my job, to . . . I . . . My wife's pregnant, she's not working any more, I . . . I'm sorry. I can't.'

Éric slunk out.

She won't ask Jean or Nathalie or anyone else. She knows when to let it drop.

The other fish are dazzlingly coloured, their scales look soft, their fins aren't damaged. They have moved away from her, they are swimming in brighter, clearer waters.

She has lost her colours, her body has become translucent, she's lying on the surface, belly up.

M athilde doesn't look at her watch, nor at the clock at the bottom of her screen, nor the one on her phone. If she starts watching the time, it will stretch into eternity.

She mustn't count anything, not the time that's gone by nor the time left to fill.

She mustn't listen to the noises coming from the other offices at the end of the corridor, sudden sounds of voices, bits of conversation in English, the ringing of the telephones.

The sound of people working.

She mustn't listen to the torrent of the flushing lavatories either. On average every twenty minutes.

Being in this place seems less difficult to her. She's got used to it.

If she thinks about it, that's all she's done since the start – get used to it. Forget how it was before, forget that things could be different, forget that she knew how to work. Get used to it and lose her way.

*

Mathilde looks at the memory stick with her personal files on it. She hesitates to put it in the slot, then gives up on the idea. Why bother transferring her files to her new computer?

Tomorrow she may be somewhere else, somewhere in the basement, near the canteen kitchens or by the bins. Or she might be transferred to another department, another subsidiary, somewhere where she'll receive calls and emails, where people will expect projects and opinions and documents from her and where she'll rediscover the desire to be there.

She presses a key on her keyboard to wake the computer. Each machine has its own memory called the C: drive. The C: drive includes 'My Documents', 'My Music' and 'My Pictures'. Her C: drive is empty since she has only just got her new machine. All the computers are linked to the company server. The server is called the M: drive. Each team has a directory on the network. The marketing and international department's directory is called MKG-INT. Everyone has to save all of their documents that relate to the team's activities there. For a few weeks, Mathilde has been looking at this directory to see the new action plans for the brands and the follow-up on promotional campaigns. She keeps herself up to date. Even if her view is no longer canvassed, even if she no longer participates, even if it is pointless.

Mathilde double-clicks on the M: drive icon. The server opens, she finds the directory and clicks again.

An error message comes up immediately:

'M:\MKG-INT\ not accessible. Access denied.'

Mathilde tries again. The same message appears.

The IT people probably forgot to configure her authorisations on her new computer.

She dials their number. She recognises the voice of the technician who came that morning, the one who asked her for her Argent Defender card.

She tells them who she is and explains her problem. She hears tapping on a keyboard, the man breathing in the handset. He's checking.

'It's got nothing to do with your new machine. You don't have authorisation to access that directory.'

'Pardon?'

'We got a memo on Friday and you're not on the list any more.'

'What list is this?'

'Each department has been asked to update its access authorisations at directory and sub-directory level . . . The request from your team doesn't give you access to this directory.'

'Who signed off on it?'

'The manager, I guess.'

'Which manager?'

'Mr Pelletier.'

There comes a moment when things have to stop. Or it's no longer possible.

She'll call him. She'll let it ring as long as necessary, twenty minutes if she has to.

But first of all she has to calm down. She has to breathe. Has to wait for her hands to stop trembling.

First she has to shut her eyes, leave the domain of anger and hatred, move away from the stream of curses that have come into her mind.

After about a hundred rings, Jacques finally picks up.

'It's Mathilde.'

'Yes?'

'Apparently you have withdrawn my authorisation to access the departmental directory.'

'Yes, that's right. Patricia Lethu told me that you've asked for a transfer. Therefore, as you know, I cannot allow you the same access as the other members of the department. You know that marketing policy obeys particular constraints of confidentiality, in-house included.'

Sometimes when she is upset her voice becomes shrill, climbing octaves in the space of a few words, but not this time. Her voice is low-pitched and composed. She is astonishingly calm.

'Jacques, we need to talk. Give me a few minutes. This is ridiculous. I wouldn't have put in for a transfer if things hadn't taken this turn, you know very well that I no longer have . . .'

'Huh . . . yes, well, listen. That's the result. We're not going to get lost going back over what happened when I think we both have better things to do.'

'No, in fact, Jacques, you know very well I have nothing to do.'

There's a silence that lasts a few seconds. Mathilde holds her breath. She glances at the Argent Defender. He is scrutinising the line of the horizon far in front of him.

Her heart is no longer beating fast. Her hands aren't trembling any more. She is calm and everything is perfectly clear. She has come to the end of something.

And then Jacques suddenly begins to shout.

'Don't talk to me in that tone of voice!'

She doesn't understand. She had spoken softly to him. Not one word louder than the rest. But Jacques is off again: 'You do not have the right to speak to me in that tone!'

She's no longer breathing. She looks around, looks for a point of anchorage, something fixed and tangible, she's looking for something that has a name, a name that no one can dispute, a shelf, a drawer, a hanging file, she's incapable of uttering a sound.

He is beside himself. He goes on: 'I forbid you to talk to me like that. You are insulting me, Mathilde. I am your line manager and you are insulting me!'

Suddenly she understands. What he's up to.

His door is wide open and he's shouting so that everyone can hear. He repeats: 'I forbid you to speak to me in that tone. What's come over you?'

Everyone can vouch for the fact that Mathilde Debord insulted him on the phone.

She's speechless. This can't be happening.

Jacques goes on. He responds to her silence with indignant exclamations, takes offence, gets enraged, exactly as though he were reacting to what she was saying. Eventually he says: 'You are becoming coarse, Mathilde. I refuse to have this conversation with you.'

He has hung up.

Then the image comes back. Jacques's face, swollen, with a trickle of blood coming from his mouth.

No, there has never been any ambiguity between her and Jacques. No misty-eyed glances or footsie under the table, no out-of-place comments, not the slightest emotion. No gestures or innuendos.

Of course people have asked her about it. They've suggested she think it over. There must have been something. All the same. For things to get out of control so suddenly and drastically. So irrationally. Something to do with feelings and desires, something she didn't want to acknowledge.

Mathilde searched her memories of those years for a detail that has escaped her. She found nothing. All the times the two of them had stayed late at the office, all the times they'd had lunch or dinner together in a restaurant, all the nights they'd spent each in their own rooms in hotels, all the hours in cars, trains and planes so close to one another, all the perfect opportunities, yet there had never been the slightest touch of skin on skin, nothing appeared on the surface that could have alerted her. It's true that once or twice at the end of the day Jacques had addressed her in the familiar form. Jacques, who addressed everyone formally. After several years, what could she conclude from that?

No, Jacques wasn't in love with her.

It was something else. From the start, he had taken her under his wing, he had got her a management job, had personally negotiated her pay rises with the management. He had made Mathilde his closest collaborator, his right hand, he had granted her the esteem with which he was so parsimonious and the trust he refused others. Because from the start he and she had agreed, without anything ever knocking it off course or getting out of control.

In her job interview Mathilde hadn't mentioned that she was a widow. She told Jacques what she told the others – that she was a single parent. That was true. She refused pity, compassion, she couldn't bear the idea that anyone had to be careful or indulgent towards her. She hated those words.

She had told him later, without going into detail. One day on the train to Marseilles in a digression from their conversation. They had been working together for over a year. Jacques behaved discreetly and didn't try to find out more. His behaviour to Mathilde didn't change and she was grateful to him for that.

Jacques's view was always broader and more far-reaching than other people's. He had an ability to anticipate, dazzling intuitions and an instinctive knowledge of the markets. They called him a visionary. From Jacques she learned everything. Beyond the technical and financial aspects, he communicated his conception of the job to her. His rigour and his demands.

Laetitia wasn't wrong. She was his creature. He had fashioned her in his image, had sensitised her to the battles that were his, had converted her to his causes. He made her a sort of disciple in flat shoes.

But he had always respected her way of seeing things and their rare differences of opinion.

He knew how much she admired him.

She saw him for what he was. Sometimes Jacques irritated her. Drove her up the wall. His sudden rages, his irony, his propensity for excess.

In Milan he called the hotel reception at two in the morning because his carpet was dirty. In fact the vacuum cleaner had brushed it up the wrong way. He told her the story the next morning himself.

In Marseilles he had sent his meal back in a restaurant with two Gault Millau stars on the grounds that the garnish looked phallic to him.

In a business hotel in Prague he called the reception-ist up to his room in the middle of the night because he couldn't find CNN among the twenty-five channels on offer.

Behind the wheel, Jacques would fulminate, he couldn't bear to wait or get stuck, he cursed at his GPS.

On planes, he always had to be at the front on the aisle, and was ready to have someone else moved to get the seat he wanted.

But Jacques had got a lot calmer. His rages had lost their intensity, their impact.

So people said.

In the past he'd made walls shake. He'd been worse in the time before she knew him, the time before her. When Jacques was commercial director. When his sarcasm reduced women to tears. When he slammed the door in the faces of colleagues. When he was capa-ble of sacking an employee in under two hours. When he hadn't yet got married.

With age, Jacques had mellowed. There remained a sort of legend about him, fed by dramatic anecdotes and rumours that were more or less verified, supported by sudden authoritarian outbursts, which he still couldn't suppress.

As far back as she could remember, Mathilde had never allowed herself to be impressed. Jacques's moods didn't interest her. And that was probably another reason why he'd liked working with her so much.

The company had been the place of her renaissance.

The company had obliged her to get dressed, do her hair, put on make-up. To get out of her torpor. To pick up the threads of her life again.

For eight years she'd gone there with a sort of enthusiasm, a kind of conviction. She'd gone with the feeling that she was useful, was making her contribution, taking part in something, was a constituent part of a whole.

The company had saved her perhaps.

She used to love the conversations in the morning around the drinks machine, the little plastic stirrers that dissolved the sugar in the coffee, the supply request forms, the timesheets, the assignment slips, she had loved the disposable propelling pencils, the highlighter pens in all sorts of colours, the correction ribbon, the notepads with squared paper and thick orange covers, the suspension files, she had loved the revolting smells from the canteen, the annual appraisal, the interdepartmental meetings, the pivot tables in Excel, the 3D graphics in PowerPoint, the collections for births and the retirement parties, she'd loved the words spoken at the same time every day, the recurring questions, the formulas emptied of meaning, the jargon particular to her team, she'd loved the ritual, the repetition. She needed it.

Today it seems to her as though the company is a crushing place.

A totalitarian place, a predatory place, a place of illusion and the abuse of power, a place of betrayal and mediocrity.

Today it seems to her that the company is a pathetic symptom of the most futile sort of mindless parroting.

Thibault got back in his car. He started it up, let off the handbrake and drove away.

He went as far as villa Brune in the fourteenth arrondissement for a case of gastro-enteritis, then to avenue Villemain for a case of nasal inflammation. Next he had to return to sector four to see someone who was unable to breathe properly, but not before he called the base to protest.

Audrey had just come on duty. She responded to his remonstrations in the same way as Rose several hours earlier: 'Thibault, things are crap today.'

She was right. Since that morning, Thibault had felt around him a kind of resistance, an unusual thickness to the air, a sense of everything slowing down but without any accompanying feeling of softening. In fact, it seemed to him now that things had been touched by some unspoken violence which the city couldn't contain.

*

He stops in front of Monoprix and checks his next address. He's much too far up. He must have driven right past it without realising. He's going to have to turn around. He sighs.

After three one-way streets, he manages to make a right. A double-parked taxi is blocking his way. He's stuck again. Inside, the driver and the passenger are deep in conversation. Thibault slips the car into neutral. He takes his foot off the clutch and shuts his eyes.

Some days are fluid: things follow one after the other like links in a chain. Then the city clears a path for him, lets him get on. And then there are days like today: chaotic and exhausted, when the city cuts him no slack at all, when he's spared nothing: not the traffic jams, nor the detours, nor the endless deliveries, nor the parking problems. Days when the city is so tense that it seems that something might happen at every junction. Something serious and irreparable.

Since this morning, now that he's alone, scattered words come back to him, trying to find meaning in the light of his failure. Now that he's alone, Lila's voice has crept inside his head, with its low, self-controlled cadences.

'Why did I meet you now?'

She's lying on her side, facing him, stroking his wrist. They've just made love for the first time. That's enough to know that they're good together. It's not a question of technique. It's a question of skin, of smell, of substance.

But right at the start, that question brings disharmony. There's so much contained in that 'now'. Now what? Now, when she still isn't over a previous affair? Now that she wants to go and live abroad? Now that she's just changed job? It doesn't matter. He'll have ample opportunity to imagine, surmise, invent. Now isn't the right time.

And then there were other words . . .

'If you manage another week, I'll buy you a toothbrush.'

'Imagine that when I got back from Geneva I said to you: let's get an apartment together and have a baby.'

'The risk isn't that I don't love you enough, it's that I love you too much.'

In these words he caught sight of her own dream, her capacity for illusion, words circumscribed by the moment and its fleeting magic, words which he had no answer for. Contradictory words divorced from reality, untranslatable.

Lila would talk in the dark after night had fallen,

or in a light alcohol-fuelled haze after she'd had a few glasses. Lila spoke as though she were singing a song written by someone else, enjoying the alliteration or the rhyme, unconnected to the meaning. Fugitive words with no consequences.

He didn't believe in this fragmentary, intermittent love, this love which could do without him for days and even weeks, this love without content.

Because Lila always had something more important to do.

It wasn't the right time. And he always came back to that: the love affair was used up before it had even happened. It was worn out from running on empty.

He wanted to be far away, to put some distance between him and it. He wished that time had already passed, the uncompressible time of suffering which he'd have to get through for six months, a year. He wanted to wake up in the autumn and feel almost like a new person, to look at the wound and see only a fine scar.

It's a matter of structuring his time until he can live again.

Killing time.

*

The sound of a horn brings him back to reality. The road ahead has cleared. Thibault goes round the block and eventually parks in front of the building where his next appointment is. He grabs his case with his left hand, which he sometimes does when he's tired.

At the age of twenty, so as not to draw attention to his disability, he gave up being left-handed. Little by little, through force of will, he learned to use his right hand. Over the course of the years, his gestures changed, his way of writing, of drinking, caressing, standing, speaking, blowing his nose, rubbing his eyes, concealing a yawn. His left hand quit the limelight. It disappeared, was folded back on itself or hidden in a sleeve. It was protected. Sometimes, though, it still reaches out when he least expects it.

As he climbs the stairs, he's thinking about that: the way things come back, return to the surface.

The paint is peeling off in strips; the yellow walls exude dampness. Above the second floor the landing lights no longer work. Before he lived here, he didn't realise that the city could be abandoned. Could be falling apart to this extent. He didn't know its ravaged face, its decrepit facades, its perfumes of dereliction. He was unaware that the city could exhale such a stink and allow itself to be gnawed away at little by little.

On the fourth floor, he knocks on the door. He waits.

He's about to knock again when he hears shuffling footsteps approaching. After several minutes, the bolts slide back.

An old woman appears in the half-open doorway. Bent double, her hands gripping her stick, she looks at him for a few seconds before opening the door completely. Her flimsy nightdress gives an indication of how thin her body is. She can barely stand.

Inside, the stench is so strong it's almost unbearable. It's a smell of old age, of closed-up rooms and refuse. From the hall, Thibault can make out the state of the kitchen. Washing up is piled in the sink and there are about ten bin bags lying on the floor.

The woman leads the way, taking small steps as she goes towards the dining room.

She invites him to sit down.

'So what's the matter, Mrs Driesman?'

'I feel tired, doctor.'

'How long have you felt that way?'

She doesn't reply.

He looks at her grey skin, her emaciated face.

She's put her hands on her knees. Suddenly Thibault thinks to himself that this woman is going to die here in front of him, that she'll go out like a light without a sound.

'Tired in what way, Mrs Driesman?'

'I don't know. I just feel very tired, doctor.'

Her mouth has entirely collapsed, her lips have disappeared.

'Don't you have dentures?'

'They fell under the basin. I can't bend down.'

Thibault gets up and goes into the bathroom. He picks up the dentures from the floor and rinses them under the tap. The floor is black with filth. On a shelf he notices an old tube of Steradent. By chance there's one tablet left. He comes back with the dentures floating in a glass. He puts it down in front of her on the oilcloth on the table.

'You can put them back in in an hour or two.'

He's seen hundreds of men and women like Mrs Driesman. Men and women whom the city harbours without even knowing it. Who end up dying at home and being found weeks later, when the smell has become too much to ignore or the maggots have worked their way through the floor.

Men and women who sometimes call the doctor simply in order to see someone. To hear another human voice. To talk for a few minutes.

Over the years, he has learned to recognise the signs of isolation. The people who go unnoticed, hidden away in shabby apartments. People no one speaks about. Because people like Mrs Driesman sometimes go for months without anyone realising that they no longer have the strength to go and collect their pensions from the post office any more.

Today something has hit him hard; he can't maintain the necessary distance between himself and this woman.

He looks at her and wants to cry.

'Do you live alone?'
  'My husband died in 2002.'
  'Do you have children?'
  'I've got a son.'
  'Does your son come to see you?'
  'He lives in London.'
  'Do you get out of the house, Mrs Driesman?'
  'Oh yes, doctor.'
  'Did you go out yesterday?'
  'No.'
  'What about the day before?'
  'No.'
  'How long has it been since you last went out?'

The woman has put her head in her hands. Her body is convulsed with sobs.

*

Apart from two cartons of condensed milk, the fridge is empty. In the cupboards, all he finds are tins of tuna and sardines. He returns to the dining room and goes over to her.

'How long has it been since you were last able to go out, Mrs Driesman?'

'I don't know.'

He listened to her chest and took her blood pressure.

He told her that his preference would be to send her to hospital long enough to sort out some follow-up with the social services. That after that she would be able to go back home and would get a daily visit from a home help.

Mrs Driesman clutched the table top with both hands. She didn't want to hear any of this. Leaving her apartment was out of the question.

He couldn't force her. He didn't have the right.

He got back in the car, having promised he'd call back tomorrow. Before he drove off, he called Audrey so that the base could file a report. A few months ago, Thibault had seen a patient in a similar condition. The old man refused to go into hospital and died of dehydration in the night.

As he turned the key in the ignition, he reflected that over the years his mistakes had coalesced to form a compact ball which he would never be rid of. A ball that would keep growing exponentially.

He's a doctor in the city: that sums up his life. He's never bought anything durable, he doesn't own an apartment or a house in the country. He has no children and isn't married. He doesn't know why. Perhaps because he doesn't have a ring finger on his left hand. No alliance is possible. He goes back to see his family only once a year.

He doesn't know why he is so far in general, so far from everything apart from his work, which monopolises all his attention. He doesn't know how the time has gone by so quickly. He will soon have been a doctor for fifteen years and nothing else has happened to him. Nothing significant.

Thibault looks at the shabby apartment block where this woman has lived for the last forty years.

He would like to go home. To draw the curtains and lie down.

His life is nothing like those of the characters in that French soap opera which was such a big hit in the 1980s. The doctors in that were brave and alert – they dashed through the night, parked on the pavement and ran up the stairs four at a time. There's nothing heroic about him. He's got his hands in the shit, and the shit sticks to them. His life does without sirens and flashing lights. His life is made up of sixty per cent cases of nasal inflammation and forty per cent loneliness. That's all his life is: a ringside view of the full scale of the disaster.

The world has closed in around her. The window-less office, the business park, the whole space. Mathilde is no longer able to think, she no longer knows what she should do and shouldn't do, what she should say and when she should keep quiet.

Her thoughts have shrivelled up.

Everything has become so small and restricted.

She can still hear Jacques's irate voice saying: 'Don't speak to me in that tone.' And his monologue which went on for several minutes, his voice loud and indignant, intended for others to hear.

Jacques has gone on the offensive. He won't let it drop. She knows him. As these ordinary hours go by, something is afoot, though she doesn't yet know what. She must guess his strategy, anticipate the next attack. Not only resist, defend yourself, Paul Vernon said.

Attack.

It's perhaps four o'clock. Or maybe not quite. In spite of herself, Mathilde counts the time that's left. She feels as though she is outside of her own body, at one remove. She can see herself, with her back against the backrest of her swivel chair, her hands flat on her desk, her head bent forward, in exactly the position she would assume if she were busy analysing data or studying a document.

Apart from the fact that all she has in front of her is a playing card.

The cupboard, the shelves, the brown stains on the carpet, the long crack above her, the halogen lamp, the coat stand askew, the position of the filing cabinet on wheels – every detail of this office has become familiar to her. In one day. She has had time to absorb it all, to put it all together, its smallest corner, its tiniest marks.

Objects don't move. They are silent. Until now, she hadn't thought about this, she hadn't realised how true this is. They have a natural propensity to become worn out, damaged, ruined. If no one touches them, moves them or takes them away. If no one touches them, protects them, covers them up.

Like them, she has been relegated to the end of a corridor, banished from the new, open spaces.

In the midst of this dead, bare world, she is the last breathing thing, the last breath. She is in the process of going extinct. What's more, that's all that's left for her to do. Melt into the background, adopt outdated shapes, press herself into them, flow into them like a fossil.

Her feet are swinging beneath her chair. She notices everything. Nothing escapes her. She's in a state of heightened, singular consciousness. Each of her gestures, each of her movements, her hand in her hair, her breathing which causes her chest to rise, the twitch of a muscle in her thigh, the slightest flicker of her eyelashes, nothing moves without her being aware of it.

Neither around her nor within her.

Time has become denser. Time has amalgamated, fused: time has become blocked at the mouth of a funnel.

She's going to leave the office. She's going to hurry across the floor, her notepad under her arm, she's going to pop up somewhere, burst in without warning, without knocking. She'll say, 'So, what's new?' or 'Where are we up to?' She'll sit down opposite Éric or Nathalie. She'll start to laugh. She'll ask how their children are. She'll arrange an extraordinary meeting, a crisis meeting. She'll declare an end to hostilities, a new era of individual creativity, she'll abolish gross margins. Or else she'll wander the corridors barefoot, stopping every so often to stroke the walls with her empty hands. She'll take the lift, press buttons at random, hum sad, nostalgic tunes. She'll ask nothing, she'll watch the others working. She'll lie down on the carpet, propped up on one elbow. She'll light a cigarette and tip the ash in the plant pots. She won't answer questions. She'll laugh when they look at her. She'll smile.

Mathilde gets up and without closing her door goes to the lift. She's going down for a breath of fresh air. To breathe. She presses the button, goes closer to the mirror to look at her face.

She looks old. Tired. She has aged ten years in a few months. She doesn't recognise herself any more.

There's nothing left of the self-possessed, confident woman she used to be.

She recognises the smokers in front of the entrance. Always the same. They go down several times a day, alone or in groups. They form a little circle around the ashtray, talking, lingering. For the first time in ages she wants a cigarette. She wants to feel the smoke burning her throat, her lungs, invading her body, anaesthetising her. She could go over to them but she keeps her distance. But not too far away. With the sun at this angle, she can only make out their silhouettes, their dark suits, light shirts and shiny shoes. She catches snippets of conversation. They're talking about ISO standards and certification procedures.

These people put on their disguise and go to the office every day. They walk in the same direction, pursue a common objective, speak the same language, inhabit the same tower, use the same lifts, eat their lunch at the same table, share the same conventions, they have a job, a pay grade, they pay social-security contributions, they save holiday and overtime, which they carry over to the next year, they collect a travel allowance and declare their net taxable income at the end of the year.

They work.

Here, spread over ten floors, there are three hundred of them.

Elsewhere there are millions.

These people in their disguise no longer recognise her. They smoke their cigarettes without even seeing her. Then they flick their stubs on the ground and go back into the building.

Back in her office, she looked at the Argent Defender. He hadn't moved. Not so much as a hair. He was standing in the same parrying posture, brandishing his shield against the enemy, braced against the wind. She thought about the balance sheet for the twentieth of May so far: Jacques had transferred her to a store cupboard without any forewarning and had hung up on her after having given the impression that she had insulted him.

The twentieth of May was a day of chaos and violence, she thought, nothing like the day that had been predicted for her.

When she went to use the computer again, it didn't respond. Neither the mouse nor the keyboard.

The fish had drowned. The screen was black.

Mathilde pressed ALT and F4 simultaneously to restart the machine. Then she waited a few seconds for it to go off before starting up the system. She thought of keyboard shortcuts, mentally listing the ones she knew, using the ALT and CTRL keys, which enabled you to copy, paste, save. She wondered if there were any comparable functions in daily life, ways of going quicker, of avoiding problems, of overriding.

She thought that the time she wasted waiting for her machine – waiting for its goodwill, its slowness, its whims – those minutes which used to horrify her, enrage her, today were comforting.

Waiting for the machine filled the time.

Mathilde is facing the screen, her hands poised above the keyboard.

An error message appears, signalled by a sort of chime. She gives a start. She reads it once and doesn't understand it at all. She reads it again:

The system DLL user32.dll was relocated in memory. The application will not run properly. The relocation occurred because the DLL C:\Windows\System32\ Hhctrl.ocx occupied an address range reserved for Windows system DLLs. The vendor supplying the DLL should be contacted for a new DLL.

She could weep. Right here and now. After all she's been through. No one would see her. No one would hear. She could sob uncontrollably, without shame, let her sorrows flood on to the keyboard, between the keys, get into the circuits. But she knows how that would end. Moments like that. When you open the box. When you let yourself go. She knows that tears bring more tears, bring old tears to mind, that they all have the same salty taste. When she cries, she misses Philippe. Philippe's absence becomes palpable within her body, begins to throb like an atrophied organ, an organ of pain.

So she rereads the message and she laughs. She laughs all alone in her windowless office.

She dials the number for computer maintenance. This time she doesn't recognise the voice of the man who replies. She asks to speak to the other one. She says, 'He's the tall fair-haired man who came this morning. With the pale blue shirt. And the glasses.'

He's on a call. They'll let him know. He'll call back as soon as possible.

She's waiting again. In this space of muted dislocation and silent collapse, amid the imminence of her own downfall.

Today, every one of her gestures and movements, each of her words, her laughter in the silence, converge on a single point: a breach in the sequence of days, a fault line from which she won't emerge unscathed.

*

She'll phone the train company. While she's waiting. She'll book tickets to go away, anywhere, at the end of term. She'll take a train to the south with the boys, she'll go to the seaside, to Nice, or Marseilles or Perpignan, it doesn't matter. She'll find a hotel or a place to rent. She needs to book the tickets, to have a fixed point of anchorage, a date that she'll write in her diary, beyond today and tomorrow, in the opaque extension of time. She checks the date of the school holidays, then dials the number.

After a few seconds of music, a woman's voice announces that she is listening. This voice doesn't belong to anyone, it comes from a highly sophisticated computer system. It's the voice you hear in every station, recognisable among thousands, a voice that pretends to be listening.

Would this voice listen to her if she said that she couldn't go on? If she said, 'I've made a mistake; get me out of here.' Would this voice listen to her if she said, 'Come and fetch me'?

The voice recognition system asks her to specify her request. Mathilde follows the instructions.

She speaks clearly, separating out the syllables. In the almost empty office, her voice echoes.

She says: 'Tickets'.

She says: 'Leisure'.

She says: 'France'.

*

She's sitting at the back of her office, speaking to someone who is no one. Someone who has the merit of answering her nicely, of getting her to repeat without becoming irritated, who doesn't start shouting, who doesn't claim that she insulted her. Someone who tells her what to do, step by step, who says: 'I didn't understand your answer' in the same patient, benevolent tone.

Someone who informs her that an adviser will be taking care of her request. Her waiting time is estimated at less than three minutes. Mathilde holds.

'Hello, SNCF, this is Nicole, how may I help you?'

This time it's a real woman. She can hardly hear her over the hubbub made by Nicole's colleagues, who all do the same thing for eight hours a day. A real woman who operates her computer and refers to herself in the third person.

Mathilde books four tickets for Marseilles, which have to be collected from the station before 9.20 a.m. on 6 June.

The real woman spells out each letter of the booking reference on her file:

'Q for Quentin, T for Thibault, M for Matthieu, F for François, T for Thibault again and A for Anatole. QTMFTA.'

*

Her holiday is known by men's first names.

Her system DLL user32.dll was relocated in memory.

The tall fair-haired chap is busy elsewhere.

The smell of Glacier Freshness is enough to make you vomit.

She's right in the middle of the world's absurdity, its lack of balance.

The man from computer maintenance has come into her office. He's wearing his mobile on his belt and there's a Stanley knife sticking out of his shirt pocket. His hair's dishevelled as though he had just appeared suddenly from the tenth floor hanging from a rope. All he needs is a cape, a long red cape billowing in the wind. You can tell from his face that the computer-maintenance man is someone who's necessary, from the furrow between his eyebrows, his preoccupied look. He can be contacted at any time, he travels ceaselessly between the ten floors, repairing, restoring, restarting. The computer-maintenance man brings help and assistance. Maybe he's related to the Argent Defender in some way that's imperceptible to the naked eye.

He's been told that Mathilde has a problem.

With a weary gesture, she points to the computer. She moves the mouse and the error message appears again.

He reassures her. It's nothing.

He'll reboot the machine. These things happen.

Mathilde moves out of the way so that he can sit down.

While he's working, she hesitates but ends up asking him the question.

'I went out for a breath of air for twenty minutes a little while ago. Do you think . . . could someone have come in while I was away . . . and tampered . . . I mean, have interfered with my computer?'

The man from computer maintenance is looking at her. The line on his forehead has deepened.

'No, no, that's got nothing to do with it. It's a config-uration problem. No, really . . . I can assure you . . .'

He falls silent and keeps working. Then he turns towards her again and his voice is gentler.

'Listen, sweetheart, if you don't mind me saying . . . maybe you . . . maybe you should get a bit of rest.'

He makes a gesture towards her, as though he were about to put his hand on her shoulder, an interrupted gesture.

Does she look so fragile? So exhausted? So devastated?

Is her fragility overflowing, going beyond her?

She looks at the man's agile hands, back on the keyboard again.

The man from computer maintenance has finished. He has rebooted the machine. The fish are back. They're bumping into each other again.

Just as he's leaving her office, Mathilde calls out to him: 'About that card . . . I'll talk to my son this evening, to see if it's possible . . . I mean for yours, your son. I'll see what we can do.'

The phone rang and Patricia Lethu's internal number flashed up.

The HR director wanted to tell her that another subsidiary in the group had a vacancy in its research centre. A senior role in the New Products and Sensory Studies department, including the direct management of a team of four. The post had been vacant for two weeks because they hadn't been able to find the ideal internal candidate. Given the economic situation, external recruitment was out. Patricia Lethu had trouble concealing her excitement.

'I've sent your CV and I called the director of the centre myself as I know him personally. I recommended you. They have one or two other candidates currently under consideration, but it seems that your profile is the best match. I was most insistent. I'll hear back very soon. He needs someone urgently. The post can't remain unfilled much longer. I didn't think it necessary to mention your current problem. That would have put you at a disadvantage. You've been with us for over eight years now, so it's perfectly legitimate that you should want a change.'

Mathilde held her breath all the time that Patricia Lethu was talking. She said yes, of course. Of course she was interested.

Her cheeks had become flushed. When she put the phone down, it seemed as though her body was working again: there was an impatience in her movements, her blood was pumping more quickly, there was a strange sort of impulse which began at the base of her spine and went all the way up to her shoulders and made her sit up straight. She could feel her heart beating even in her wrists and in the veins of her neck.

She got up from her chair. She needed to move around. She paced her office and for a few minutes she didn't hear any of the noises, not the torrent of the flush nor sounds of voices.

Mathilde needed more fresh air. She went back down in the lift; after all, what did it matter?

She remained outside for a moment, with her eyes closed and her face to the light. Above her rose the glass pyramid, so smooth-looking.

Another group had come out for a smoke. Among them she recognised some people from management control and admin. They greeted her. A young woman took a cigarette from her packet and turned to Mathilde to offer her one. After a moment's hesitation, Mathilde said no. The young woman didn't rejoin the others but stayed near Mathilde, on the other side of the entrance. The young woman asked which department she worked in, how long she'd been there. If she had tried the lunchtime gym class, if she knew a swimming pool nearby, if she lived far away. She was wearing a light dress with a geometric pattern and wedge heels.

Her name was Elizabeth. She'd been working for the company for a month.

Elizabeth was happy to be here, that's what she said. She'd found her 'dream job'. For a few seconds, Mathilde envied Elizabeth, with her youth and her confidence. Her way of combining a certain capriciousness with her feelings. She thought that she'd like to be in her position, wearing that dress, with those fine hands, that same ease, her fluid way of moving and of standing. And that it would be infinitely easier if she were someone else.

As Elizabeth went off with her colleagues, she said, 'See you.'

'Hope I see you again.'

That was strange. This woman had come over to her, had spoken to her. She had asked her questions and laughed.

Mathilde went back up in the lift. When she got back to room 500–9, it didn't seem so small any more.

S he'd just sat back down when her phone rang again. It was the director of the research centre. He had looked at her CV and wanted to meet her as soon as possible. Would tomorrow work?

She didn't know by what miracle or desperate mustering of her remaining resources, by what last effort or burst of energy, she managed to respond calmly to his questions. And, it seemed to her, with relative self-assurance; not like someone who's pretending to be mentally healthy, but someone for whom nothing more than a possible transfer is at stake.

She was able to describe her projects, her responsibilities and her main achievements to him exactly as though they still existed, as though they had never slipped away from her. She forgot about the nine empty months, a vague gap in the continuity of time. She rediscovered words that she no longer used, the appropriate vocabulary, deliberate, proactive phrases; she mentioned figures, budget totals and didn't make any mistakes.

*

The director of the research centre knew of her; he'd really enjoyed her articles in the group journal.

'I confess that I used to look out for your name! It's a pity you don't write any more, but I suppose you don't have the time. We're all in the same position: nose to the grindstone. Well, I'd be delighted to see you tomorrow if you'd like to meet. I'll be in a meeting all afternoon, so would half past six suit you?'

There was something straightforward in the way he spoke to her, a sort of kindness.

She put her Paris transport map on the desk in front of her to work out how to get there. She studied the distance between the research centre and home, considered the different options, calculated the journey time. It wasn't far. Half an hour at the most.

She'd wear her grey suit, or maybe her black one, set it off with a red scarf. She wouldn't have coffee after lunchtime. She'd leave at around half five to make sure she wasn't late. She'd make herself smile, wouldn't talk about Jacques, would avoid any reference to working with him, explicit or implicit. She'd talk about her own successes, the repositioning of the L. brand, the launch of the B. food supplements, the recent loyalty scheme. She'd iron her white blouse. She'd get up earlier than usual. She'd avoid subjects that risked making her get emotional. She'd mention the creation of a consumer panel, the test products she put in place a few years ago. She won't cross her legs, will put on clear nail varnish, won't talk about her children unless he asks. She'll use verbs of action and avoid the conditional and any phrases that smack of passivity or a wait-and-see attitude. She'll sit up straight, she'll . . .

Mathilde had been deep in her strategic planning for a while when a chime announced the arrival of an email in her inbox. The director of the research centre's assistant had sent her confirmation of their meeting along with a map of the site. The email had been sent with high priority, which she noticed at once and felt touched.

She remained motionless for several minutes in front of the screen. A possibility was opening up before her and it seemed real.

She thought that her life might get back on track. That she would become herself again, make expansive gestures again, regain the pleasure of going to work and coming back home. She would no longer spend hours lying in the dark with her eyes wide open. Jacques would depart from her nights as quickly as he had come into them. She would once again have stories to tell the children. She'd take them to the swimming pool and the ice rink; she'd invent meals from leftovers again and give them funny names; she'd spend whole afternoons with them at the library.

She thought that life would recover that sweetness. That nothing was lost.

She thought she'd buy a flat-screen for their DVD evenings and would renew her membership of the film club. She thought she'd invite her friends over for dinner. They could celebrate her transfer with champagne. Maybe they'd push back the furniture and dance in her little living room. Like they used to.

She couldn't wait for it to be tomorrow.

She had the courage to go. She could do it.

She called Théo and Maxime to make sure that they'd got home OK, and then she rang Simon on his mobile to remind him not to take too long because his brothers were home alone.

She called her mother, as she'd left her several messages over the last few days which she hadn't responded to. She talked about the boys; they were fine, yes, the twins were getting ready for a school trip to the seaside and Simon had got his brown belt in judo. Her mother said: 'You sound in good form.' She promised to call her back at the end of the week.

*

On the way home this evening she'll buy some fish, or maybe a chicken, and some little fruit tarts for dessert.

She'll give this evening a foretaste of celebration, without telling the children about it, just to see their eyes light up. Just to give herself strength.

S he visited the research centre's website, took notes and prepared questions.

In her cardboard boxes she found several market studies and various thoughts on strategic analysis which she'd written under her own name in the past two years. She made a list, with on one side all the points in favour of her application, the obvious transferable skills, and on the other the skills that she would have to acquire. The balance was in her favour.

She gave a start when the phone rang.

Patricia Lethu wanted to clarify that, in the event of Mathilde being appointed, she would do all she could to see that her transfer went through at once. Given the circumstances.

She imagined a new life, new faces, a new setting. New possibilities.

She imagined a sort of sweetness; poetic justice.

When Thibault got back into his car for the tenth time, his next appointment had come up on his mobile. He didn't pull off. Sitting there, he had an uncontrollable desire to go to sleep, all of a sudden. He would have been content to slump against the headrest. He waited for a few minutes with his hand on the key and then he got out again. A queue had formed at the baker's all along the window. He had no idea what time it was. People were beginning to emerge from their offices, walking quickly.

He went into the nearest bar and ordered a coffee. He sent a text to say that he was taking a break.

He looked around. For weeks he'd been observing men. The way they spoke, how they stood, the brand of clothes they wore, the shape of their shoes. And in every case, having examined him under the magnifying glass, he wondered if Lila could fall in love with a man like that. And whether she would be capable of loving *him* if he were more handsome, taller, more classically good-looking, more voluble, more arrogant.

For weeks, he wasted his time with speculation and conjecture. He looked for what was wrong with him, what it was about him that jarred.

But no longer. He's not looking at anyone. He's breathing again.

He's left Lila. He's done it. It feels as though it's less painful. Over the past few hours, something has become calmer. Perhaps, like a candle starved of oxygen, it will end up going out entirely. Perhaps a moment comes when you realise you've avoided the worst. A moment when you regain confidence in your own ability to pull yourself together, to rebuild yourself.

He feels better. He orders another coffee.

He's going to make it. Two or three more appointments and the day will be over.

Next weekend he'll buy himself a flat-screen for his DVD evenings. And then he'll invite his university friends, the ones who've settled in Paris whom he never sees because he works too much. He'll organise a little get-together at home. He'll buy things to eat and drink. And maybe they'll push the furniture aside and dance in the living room. Like they used to.

He puts his money down on the counter and leaves.

*

When he first moved here, he wasn't yet thirty. He wanted to practise his profession, tackle the mystery of diseases, lose himself in the city. He wanted to discover the extent of injuries, the chance of disorders, how deep wounds go.

He wanted to see everything and he has seen it. Probably all he has to do now is start living.

Patricia Lethu was speaking quickly in a low voice. Her words ran into each other, such was the extent of her agitation. Patricia Lethu had been overtaken by events. Mathilde visualised her at the back of her office, with the door closed, hunched over the receiver, one hand in front of her mouth to stop her voice from carrying. Mathilde asked her to repeat it several times. She was having trouble hearing.

Patricia Lethu had to ring off quickly. She had a call on the other line. She said, 'I'll come and see you right way. Don't do anything until I see you.'

Jacques Pelletier had asked the HR director to send Mathilde, by recorded delivery, a warning letter which he had written himself. In it, he mentioned the repeated instances of verbal aggression which he had been subjected to, the insults she had hurled at him and the fact that Mathilde had slammed the phone down on him several times. He complained about her systematic opposition to the direction and strategy of the business and described, with the aid of several examples, her self-inflicted isolation and refusal to communicate with others.

Patricia Lethu read extracts in a hushed voice, with the letter in front of her.

The warning didn't entail disciplinary measures, she thought it helpful to make clear. But it would be kept on her file. And it could be a determining factor in a dismissal procedure over a mistake or suspension.

Moreover, Jacques had formally opposed a transfer of any sort. The loss of a manager would put the whole team at risk. He refused to contemplate Mathilde's departure until a new person had been recruited and trained. In his view, no transfer could be considered for four or five months.

Patricia Lethu repeated: 'Don't do anything until I see you.'

Unlike the fish, which have resumed their dance on either side of the screen, the Argent Defender is stationary. He's waiting for the right moment, refining his strategy.

The Argent Defender isn't the type to rush into action without taking time to reflect.

Mathilde glances at the clock on the computer. It's 5.45. She tries to reconstruct the factors mentioned by

Patricia Lethu, she jots down the words she remembers on a pad of squared paper, then strikes them through and tears up the paper. She cannot believe it.

From the start, all of this can only have belonged to a dream. All of it comes from a B-movie nightmare, a shock of fear in the middle of the night, which is fruitless and doesn't free you from anything. A nightmare like the ones she used to have as a child, when she dreamed that she had forgotten to get dressed and found herself standing in the middle of the playground in the nude, a source of general hilarity.

So a moment must come when she'll wake up, when she'll grasp the division between reality and sleep, and realise that that is all this was: a long nightmare. When she'll experience the intense relief that follows the return to consciousness, even if her heart is still beating fit to explode, even if she is bathed in sweat in her darkened bedroom. A moment when she will be free.

But all this has happened since the start. It can all be analysed, dissected, step by step. This pitiless mechanism, her great naïveté and the countless tactical blunders she has made.

*

She is Jacques Pelletier's deputy. The title appears on her last payslip and in the company's organisation chart.

His adjunct: joined to him.

Linked.

Bound hand and foot.

He's not going to let her escape, allow her to free herself so easily from the hold he has over her.

He's well aware that she can be replaced. At the point they have reached. For months he has behaved in a way that has enabled him to do without her, to bypass her. For months he has been putting in place a structure that works without her, even if he himself has had to work twice as hard. You only have to look at his face, the dark circles round his eyes. He knows full well that he could find a hundred others if he needed to, younger, more dynamic, more malleable. Corinne Santoses by the bucketful falling from the sky.

She has come to the end of a long spiral after which there is nothing. When she thinks about it, given the logical way things have unfolded, their progressive, unstoppable escalation, there is nothing more. What more can he do to harm her? What further warnings or humiliations?

Whatever she does, whatever she says, she loses.

*

Mathilde's gaze wanders in empty space. Her gestures no longer exist. Not the pen travelling across the paper, nor the cup she brings to her lips, nor the hand that opens the drawer.

Since she's lost everything, she no longer has anything left to lose.

Since Jacques has shown himself to be economical with the truth, she will show him the meaning of the word 'insult'.

There, that's settled.

She'll go into his office and hurl, heap, *pour* insults on him, give him a dazzling display of how rich her vocabulary is; in fact she begins to make an inventory of it.

She'll speak to him in *that tone*, and much worse besides. She'll speak to him in a tone that he won't even be able to imagine, whose very existence he will be unaware of, she'll speak to him as no one has ever spoken to him. She'll go into his office, shut the door behind her and the words will come out of her in a single compact mass without drawing breath, without a gap that would enable him to take her to task, an uninterrupted stream of insults. She will spit vipers and toads in his face, like a princess in a fairy tale, in the thrall of a terrible fate, waiting to be rescued . . .

*

Mathilde gets up and goes to Jacques's office. She imagines the relief, is anticipating it.

In this impulse which propels her towards him, the images come back. The long gash in Jacques's body, his hair plastered to his forehead, the fear in his eyes, his blood soaking into the carpet.

J acques is in front of her. In the corridor.

He's carrying his bag in his right hand, standing by the lift. The call button is flashing. Office doors around him are open. Through the glass of the open-plan area Mathilde can see the others, trying to look busy, but watching, she can tell. They're hoping for thunder and lightning, fireworks.

She hadn't expected to find him there, ready to leave. She had imagined seeing him in his office, away from people's eyes. She can't let out a stream of abuse here in front of everybody. The stream would become a puddle.

'Jacques, I need to talk to you.'

'I don't have time.'

After a few seconds, she adds: 'You can't do this. We have to talk.'

He doesn't reply.

She goes up to him. She feels the veins in her temples

throbbing. For a moment she thinks she's going to throw up, right here at his feet.

'Don't do this.'

A bell announces the arrival of the lift. He goes in, presses o and turns towards her. He looks her straight in the eye. She has never before seen such a harsh look on his face.

The doors close. He's gone.

'Oh no, Mr Pelletier won't be back today, nor tomorrow. He's away for four days and won't be in the office till next week. Is there anything I can do to help?'

Corinne Santos's heady perfume seems to have impregnated the furniture, the carpet and every cubic inch of air, as though this office has been hers since the dawn of time. Mathilde dislikes everything about this woman: her affected manner, her pretentious way of speaking, the red plastic balls on her necklace. Mathilde hates her. She feels angry with herself for hating her so much. To want so badly to tear up her papers, to mess up her hair, to spit in her face. She wishes that Corinne Santos were even more pathetic, repulsively vulgar, that her errors, gaffes and mistakes would mount up, that she would demonstrate spectacular incompetence, that she would be caught with Jacques in a position strongly suggestive of fellatio, and that the news would go all round the company in under two hours, that the two of them would become the subject of the most malicious gossip. She would like Corinne Santos to disintegrate here before her eyes, or deflate or dissolve into dust.

Mathilde can make out her own reflection in the window. Rigid.

She is like him. Like all of them. Just as mediocre. Just as petty.

The company has turned her into this mean-minded, unfair creature.

The company has made her this creature of rancour and bitterness, desperate for revenge.

She left Corinne Santos's office without another word. She went past the copy room to pick up a packet of paper. She returned to her lair, tore at the packaging and grabbed a white sheet.

In the top left she wrote her address. On the right, Patricia Lethu's name and that of the company.

Subject: Letter of resignation
Receipt acknowledged by _____

Madam,
By this letter I wish to inform you of my intention to resign from the position of deputy marketing director, which I have held since 7 January 2001.

In view of the context, I would be grateful if you would waive my notice period.

I thank you in advance for informing me as soon as possible of the official date of my last day at work.

Mathilde crumples it up, throws it away and starts again.

Subject: Letter of resignation

Madam,
I am hereby ending our collaboration and by this letter confirm my resignation from your company. I would like my resignation to be effective from 22 May 2009.

I remain at your disposal for any additional information.
Yours sincerely,

It's her last recourse. She knows that.

It's what she should avoid at all costs. Come what may.

The thing you must never ever do. Never.

But there comes a moment when the price is too high. When it's more than you can afford. A time when you must quit the game, accept that you've lost. There comes a time when you can't stoop any lower.

S he's sitting down. She stretches her legs out in front of her.

It's over.

She must get up, tidy her things into a bag, put on her jacket and leave the office. She must manage to leave the building and walk to the station. She must hand-deliver her letter to Patricia Lethu or else stop at the post office and send it recorded delivery.

For the moment, she doesn't move. She can't move. Her body has abandoned her for a few seconds, become disconnected.

When Patricia Lethu came into the office, Mathilde handed her the letter without saying anything. The HR director opened the envelope and looked stunned. Mathilde asked her to sign where it said 'receipt acknowledged by'.

During Patricia Lethu's silence, Mathilde thought that compassion only occurs when you see yourself in the other's shoes, when you realise that everything that is happening to someone else could happen to you, exactly the same, with the same violence and brutality.

In this awareness that you're not protected, that you too could sink so low – and only there – compassion can arise. Compassion is nothing but a fear on your own behalf.

After a few moments, Patricia Lethu signed where Mathilde had indicated.

'If tomorrow or in the future you want to go back on this decision, I will consider that I have never had this letter in my hands.'

'But you have had it and you've just signed it.'

'But you're exhausted, Mathilde. You need to rest. We'll find a solution. I'll speak to him. At least wait until I've talked to him.'

'I need you to take this letter on board. To regard it as final and irrevocable.'

'As you wish. But let's talk again. You look very pale. I want you to take a taxi home. And call an emergency doctor. Make yourself stop for a few days, a week. You're at the end of your tether.'

'I'm taking the train.'

'Take a taxi and charge it. You're in no fit state to go home on public transport.'

'I'm going to take the train.'

'OK. But promise me you'll call a doctor as soon as you get home. Mathilde, you need to stop. Promise me. You're not going to be able to keep going.'

'I'll call a doctor.'

The two of them stayed like that face to face in silence. Mathilde didn't have the strength to get up, she needed to wait till her body adjusted, till it found support. The offices were half-empty, the noise around them had faded.

After a few minutes Mathilde asked: 'Are we responsible for what happens to us? Do we always get what we deserve?'

'What do you mean?'

'Do you think a person becomes a victim of something like this because she's weak, because that's what she wants, because, even if this seems incomprehensible, she has chosen it? Do you believe that certain people, without knowing it, mark themselves out as targets?'

Patricia Lethu pondered for a moment before answering.

'No, I don't think so. I think it's your capacity to resist that marks you out as a target. I've been in this business for thirty years, Mathilde, and this isn't the first time I've encountered this sort of situation. You're not responsible for what's happening to you.'

'I'm going home.'

Patricia Lethu gets up. Her bracelets clinking together sound like little bells.

As she goes to the door, she repeats: 'Call a doctor.'

He drove onto the Tolbiac bridge. Halfway across, stopped by a red light, he turned to look at the river, at the metallic colour of the water sparkling in the pale light. The geometry of the other bridges shaded off into the distance, a sequence of long or rounded shapes, light and pure, as far as the eye could see.

There were moments like this, when the city took his breath away. When the city gave, asking nothing in return.

A few minutes later, on the quai François Mauriac, he passed the brand-new building where he had his next appointment. The address belonged to an international consultancy firm. Unless he used the company car park, he had no chance of finding anywhere to leave the car. He drove round the block as a matter of principle and then went down into the tunnel that led to the first underground level. He explained to the attendant that he was a doctor and had an appointment. The man refused to raise the barrier. No one had informed him. Only visitors he'd been told about with a pre-booked parking place had access to the car park. Thibault explained the situation again. He wouldn't be long, there was nowhere else to park within half a mile. He made a point of breathing after each sentence so as not to lose his temper. The attendant shook his head.

That was when Thibault wanted to get out of his car and drag him out of his box by his collar and press the button himself. Suddenly he could visualise himself doing exactly that: hurling the man on to the middle of the concrete ramp.

He closed his eyes for just a second. He didn't move.

He turned off his engine and demanded that the man call his patient, who as it turned out was one of the company directors.

Ten minutes later – by which time there were several cars stuck behind him – the man finally opened the barrier.

Thibault gave his name at reception. The receptionist asked him to fill in a visitor form and to be so kind as to leave his identity card.

As she was very pretty, he didn't get annoyed.

As he noticed that she was very pretty, he told himself that he wasn't dead yet.

While the young woman was letting Mr M. know that his visitor had arrived – exactly as though Thibault was some tradesman – he turned his phone to silent. With a polite smile, the receptionist handed him a badge with his name on it.

A man in a dark suit was waiting for him in a vast office full of designer furniture that looked as though it had just been unpacked. The man, who had a pallid complexion and dark-shadowed eyes, came over to shake his hand.

Thibault reflected that some men of his age looked worse than him. That was reassuring.

'Hello, doctor. Do sit down.'

The man indicated a black leather armchair. Thibault remained standing.

'I've had a very painful throat infection since yesterday. I need antibiotics. I respond well to Amoxicillin, or Zithromax if you prefer.'

Every week he sees overworked managers who have emergency doctors come to their offices so as not to waste a minute. It's one of the ways in which his job has changed, along with the ever-increasing rise in stress-related conditions: lumbago, neck pain, intestinal and gastric trouble and other musculoskeletal problems. He knows these people by heart – the over-performers, the high-flyers, the competitive ones. The ones who never stop. He also knows the opposite, the flipside of the coin, the moment when things slide, when one knee goes down, the moment when something creeps in which they hadn't foreseen, when something kicks off that they can't control, the moment when they go over to the other side. He sees these ones every week too – the men and women who are exhausted, dependent on sleeping pills, like blown bulbs or drained batteries. Men and women who call on a Monday morning because they can't take any more.

He knows how weak and fragile the border between the two states is, and that a person can crumble more quickly than they would believe.

He's happy to be flexible. Make an effort.

He's happy to spend ten minutes negotiating with a stubborn parking attendant in order to get into a car park and ten minutes more waiting for a plastic badge that he won't wear to be printed.

But he cannot bear people who want to tell him what to prescribe.

'If you'll allow me, I'd like to listen to your chest.'

The man can't suppress a sigh.

'Listen, doctor, I've had a fair number of throat infections and my next meeting starts in four minutes.'

Thibault forces himself to stay calm. But his voice, he realises, betrays his irritation.

'Sir, most throat infections are viral in origin. Antibiotics are useless. As I'm sure you know, misusing antibiotics increases resistance, which poses a serious health risk both to individuals and the general public.'

'I couldn't give a damn. I need to be better in twenty-four hours.'

'You won't get better any quicker with an inappropriate treatment.'

He couldn't stop himself raising his voice.

The last time he refused to prescribe antibiotics, the guy threw his case out the window.

Thibault looks around: here, thanks to the air conditioning, the windows don't open.

Why does he dislike this man so much? Why does this man make him want to get the better of him, to have the last word? Why does he want to see this man give in?

This is what he has sunk to, at 6 p.m.: an excess of testosterone, all puffed up like a little cockerel.

He'd like to go home and lie down.

The man is standing in front of him, challenging him.

'How much do I owe you?'

'Thirty-four euros.'

'That's a lot for a three-minute consultation and no prescription.'

'Listen, sir, I won't write a prescription without listening to your chest.'

Mr M. isn't used to giving in. He folds the cheque and drops it on the carpet at Thibault's feet.

Without taking his eyes off him, Thibault bends down and picks it up.

As he goes to the lift, he thinks: I hope he croaks in his office.

S he looked up the emergency doctor's number on the Internet. She told herself that she would call before she left and get a doctor to make a house call after 7 p.m.

She dialled the number. Just as the operator answered, Éric went past her door. Mathilde was afraid he'd hear her conversation from the toilets. She hung up.

She waited a bit. Just as she redialled the number, her mobile rang. She hung up again and picked up the other phone. She was tired. An operator from Bouygues Telecom wanted to know why she had changed service provider a year ago. She could no longer remember. The operator wanted to know when her contract with her new service provider ended and in what circumstances she'd consider returning to Bouygues Telecom. Just as the operator was getting ready to run through various offers so that she could choose the one that appealed the most, Mathilde began to cry.

Émilie Dupont read out response number 12 as fast as she could: Bouygues Telecom thanked Mathilde for her kind attention and would call back at a more suitable time to suggest some new offers.

It was raining when Mathilde left the building, a light rain made dirty by the nearby factories, a rain soiled by the world's waste, she thought. The pavement seemed to give way beneath her, or else it was her legs which were folding under the weight of having given up. It was as though she were imperceptibly subsiding into the ground, as if her body no longer knew how to remain upright. At one moment she could see herself collapsing on the asphalt through a sort of short-circuit. And yet she didn't.

That song came back to her, the one she and Philippe loved so much. 'On and on, the rain will fall, like tears from a star, on and on, the rain will say, how fragile we are, how fragile we are . . .' She thought how she was a grey shape among millions of others, gliding over the tarmac. She thought how slow she was. Before, she would have practically run to the station, even on four-inch heels, hurrying to catch the VOVA at 6.40 p.m.

The brasserie was closed. From outside she could see the smooth, empty counter and chairs on tables. She wondered if Bernard had maybe gone on holiday. Everything seemed so clean. She had seen him that very morning and again at lunchtime. Maybe he'd told her and she hadn't been listening.

At the same moment a man was coming towards her, he was getting off his scooter. He removed his helmet. He wanted to ask her for a drink or a coffee. He was persistent. He said: 'Please. You're wonderful!'

Suddenly Mathilde wanted to cry. To cry again without holding back in front of this man so that he would realise that she wasn't wonderful at all. Quite the reverse, she was nothing but rubbish, a faulty part rejected by the whole, a piece of residue. He kept on at her: 'The way you look, your hair. I'd really love to ask you for a drink.'

The man was handsome. He was smiling.

She said, 'I'm not in great shape at the moment,' and he replied, 'Well, there you are then! It would do you good, it'd take your mind off it.'

She kept walking, with him following her. He ended up proffering his card and saying:

'Call me. Some other time. When you feel like it. I've seen you around. I know you work nearby. Call me. You've got all my numbers.'

She slipped the card into her pocket. She made an effort to smile. She left him there.

He was holding his helmet in his hand, watching her go.

*

Since Philippe's death she's met other men. A few. Perhaps you only love once. *In love there are no refills.* She read that sentence in a book once a long time ago and scarcely paused over it. A tiny resonance. But the phrase came back to her each time she broke up with a man she'd thought she loved. For ten years she's had affairs in the margins of her life, just on the edge, without her children knowing. And ultimately she couldn't care less about the affairs. Every time the question of sharing their furniture and their time has come up, of following the same path, she's left. She can't take it. Maybe it could only happen in the heedlessness of being a twenty-year-old: living together, in the same place, breathing the same air, sharing the same bed every day, the same bathroom. Yes, maybe that happens only once, and afterwards nothing like that is possible. You can't start again.

Mathilde gets to the station and looks up at the electronic display. She's just missed the train. The next one's been cancelled.

Of all the lines in the Île-de-France, line D on the RER probably holds the record for technical failures, industrial action, mad passengers, gallons of urine, incomprehensible announcements and wrong information.

She's going to have to wait half an hour. Standing up.

*

233

She goes up the stairs to platform B. The waiting room was demolished several months ago. On the ground you can still make out the footprint of where it once stood.

SNCF has got rid of all closed shelters throughout the Île-de-France to stop the homeless using them. That's what someone told her.

A bit further down the platform a sort of giant toaster was installed at the beginning of the winter. Its red, burning elements gave out heat three feet all around. When it was cold, passengers gathered there, holding out their hands to warm them. On this spring evening, through some sort of strange conditioning, they are clustered around it even though it is turned off.

Mathilde has just resigned. She is feeling neither regret nor relief. Perhaps a sensation of emptiness.

Mathilde is standing by herself, watching people, the tiredness on their faces, that look of upset, the bitterness in their lips. The FOVA has been cancelled. They're going to have to wait. It seems to her that she shares with them something which other people are unaware of. Nearly every evening side by side they wait for trains with absurd names in this giant rush of air. And yet this doesn't bring them together, doesn't create any link.

*

Mathilde takes out the card which the man gave her a short while ago. His name is Sylvain Bourdin. He's in sales and marketing. He works for a company called Pest Control. Under the logo, in italic letters, the company mission is spelled out: 'The eradication of pests, bed bugs, lice, cockroaches, mice, rats, pigeons. Insect extermination. Disinfection.'

Mathilde feels laughter in her stomach, like a wave. But it stops at once. If she weren't so tired she would laugh heartily, uproariously. The man on the twentieth of May is a professional exterminator who gets rid of undesirables.

She didn't recognise him. She went past him. She refused to go for a drink. She didn't stop.

It's not that simple. Every time he gets into his car, Lila's perfume turns his stomach. Even though he's left the windows half open since this morning. When he leans over to the passenger side, the perfume is even stronger, it's ingrained.

He'll get the inside of the car cleaned. Next weekend.

He remembers that night when he went over to Lila's place very late. She'd called him around midnight and asked him to come, right away. He was hardly through the door when she started undressing him. They made love without speaking. And then they lay down on the bed side by side. In the darkness the whiteness of her body seemed phosphorescent. Lila's breathing had grown calmer little by little. He thought she was asleep. Once again he felt dispossessed, dispersed. Alone.

And then by some strange instinct in the silence he touched her face. Her face was wet with tears. He held her hand on top of the sheet.

He didn't know how to love her. He didn't know how to make her laugh, to make her happy.

He loved her with his doubts, his despair, he loved her from the darkest part of himself, the heart of his fault lines, in the throbbing of his own wounds.

He loved her with the fear of losing her, all the time.

The message from the base mentioned a thirty-two-year-old woman with mild neurological symptoms. The appointment was classified as moderately urgent.

Thibault wasn't sure where the street was. He got his map out of the glove compartment. It was 6.35. With a bit of luck, this would be his last appointment. It took him nearly twenty-five minutes to get there. In front of the building, a delivery space had just been vacated as he arrived.

He took the lift and walked along an endless corridor with rendered walls. He looked for the right number among the ten or so doors on that floor. He rang the bell.

The young woman is sitting in front of him. He notices her long legs, the strange lopsided way she has of sitting on her chair, her freckles and the few strands which have escaped from her pinned-up hair. She possesses an unusual beauty which moves him.

She told him the story. From the beginning.

A few days earlier, when she was working on the computer, her hand suddenly stopped working. Her hand was on the mouse and she could no longer hold or move it. And then it went back to normal. Later that evening, again while she was working, a black veil obscured her vision. For a few seconds she couldn't see anything. She wasn't too worried. She put it down to tiredness. Two days later she missed her step on the stairs, exactly as though her body were disconnected from her brain for a split second.

And then this morning, the coffee pot fell at her feet without her understanding why. She'd been holding it in her left hand and let it go. That's when she called.

She doesn't have a GP. She's never ill.

She's standing in front of him, her hands joined on the table. She asks him if it's serious. And then she adds: 'I want to know exactly what you're thinking.'

Thibault did a full neurological examination.

He is going to have to convince her to have more extensive tests without delay. He is going to have to convince her without panicking her. This woman is thirty-two years old and is presenting the first symptoms of multiple sclerosis or a brain tumour. That's what he's thinking.

'It's too soon to say. But you must take these signs very seriously. As your condition seems to have returned to normal, I'm not going to ask for you to be hospitalised. But tomorrow you must make appointments for the tests I'm going to prescribe. I'll call the hospital myself so that you're seen as quickly as possible. And if something else happens before then, you must go to casualty.'

She doesn't press him. She looks at him and smiles.

He wants to go over to her and take her in his arms. To rock her and tell her not to worry.

He wants to stroke her cheek, her hair. To tell her that he's there with her, that he won't leave her.

He's seen hundreds of patients with serious illnesses. He knows the way life collapses and how quickly. He's familiar with overdoses, heart attacks, sudden cancers and the constant suicide figures. He knows you can die at thirty.

But this evening, facing this woman, that seems intolerable.

This evening he feels as though he has lost his layer of protection, that invisible distance without which it is impossible for him to pursue his profession. He's missing something, there's something he lacks.

This evening he is naked.

*

He looks for the switch on the landing and turns on the light.

The young woman waves again, thanks him. She closes the door behind him.

He sits in his car. He's unable to drive off.

For a long time, in the absence of God, he has looked for a higher reason in illness.

Something which would give him a meaning.

Something which would justify the fear, the suffering, the flesh eaten into, exposed, the hours of immobility.

But he's no longer looking. He knows how blind and pointless illness is. He is familiar with how fragile the body is.

And against that, ultimately he can do nothing.

For the first time in ages he wants to smoke a cigarette. He wants to feel the smoke burn his throat, his lungs, invade his body, numb him.

He notices a card slipped under his windscreen wiper.

He gets out of the car and removes it. He sits back down again to read it.

'Mr Salif, medium, can resolve your most desperate problems in 48 hours. If your girl/boyfriend has left you, he/she will come running back like a dog after its master. Speedy return of the loved one. Affection rediscovered. Spells broken. Luck. Work. Sexual power. Success in all fields. Exams, driving tests.'

He feels laughter in his stomach, like a wave. But it stops at once. If he weren't so tired he would laugh heartily, uproariously. Thibault throws the card out the window. He couldn't care less about the city and its dirt. Today he could quite cheerfully empty into the gutter all the crumpled papers and empty wrappers that have littered the floor of his car for weeks. He could spit on the ground and leave his engine idling for hours. He doesn't give a fuck.

The base called to ask him if he could go to the police station in the thirteenth arrondissement for an arrest. The cops had been waiting two hours for a medical certificate for a minor.

He said no.

He has no desire to go and examine some sixteen-year-old kid who's just stuck another kid with a blade to confirm that he's in a fit state to be detained by the police.

It's beyond him.

He remembers in the early days the time he would spend at his window, watching people, the attentive hours spent in cafés when he dined alone, listening to other people, guessing their stories. He loved this city, the tangle of its stories, these shapes multiplied to infinity, the countless faces. He loved the effervescence, the crossed destinies, the sum of the possibilities.

He loved that moment when the city grows calm and the strange rumble of the asphalt when night falls, as though the street were giving back the violence it's absorbed, its excess emotion.

It seemed to him then that there was nothing more beautiful, more dizzying than this great mass of humanity.

Now he sees three thousand patients a year, he knows their irritations, their loose coughs and their dry coughs, their addictions and their migraines and their insomnia.

He knows their loneliness.

Now he knows how brutal the city is and the high price it exacts from those who expect to survive there.

And yet he wouldn't leave for anything in the world.

He's forty-three. He spends a third of his time in his car looking for a parking place or stuck behind delivery trucks. He lives in a big two-room apartment above the place des Ternes. He's always lived alone, apart from a few months when he was a student. None the less he has known a certain number of women and some of them loved him.

He hasn't known how to put down his bags and stop moving.

He's left Lila. He's done it.

You can't make other people love you. That's what he repeats to himself, to justify his actions.

At other times perhaps he would have fought.

But not now. He's too tired.

There comes a moment when the price becomes too high. Exceeds your resources.

When you have to get out of the game, accept you've lost. There comes a moment when you can't stoop any lower.

He's going to go home.

He'll pick up his mail in the letter box, climb up five floors. He'll make himself a gin and tonic and put on a CD.

He'll take stock of precisely what he's done. He'll be able to cry, even if just to show he's still capable of it. Blow his nose noisily, drown his sorrows in alcohol, kick his shoes off on his IKEA carpet, give in to the stereotype, wallow in it.

A voice was asking passengers to stand back from the edge of the platform, as the train drew slowly into the station. Mathilde got into the second carriage so that she could get off near the escalators when she reached the gare de Lyon.

With her forehead against the window, she's watching the apartment blocks alongside the track go by, with their half-open curtains, underpants on the line, symmetrical flower pots, a child's tractor abandoned on a balcony, these tiny lives, reduced, uncountable. Further on, the track crosses the Seine. She makes out the pagoda-shaped Chinese hotel and the smoke from the factories in Vitry.

On the train home, people take stock of their day, they sigh, unwind, grumble, exchange indiscretions. When the information is really confidential, they lean closer to each other, lower their voices, sometimes they laugh.

*

She closes her eyes. She listens to the conversations around her, she listens without seeing, eyelids shut. She remembers the hours she spent lying on the beach as a child, without moving, soothed by the high-pitched cries and the noise of the sea going out, surrounded by voices without faces. 'Don't leave your wet swimsuits on the sand.' 'Martine, put your hat on.' 'Stay in the shade.' 'Come and get your sandwiches.' 'Who left the cool box open?'

She used to be in the habit of reading, but she hasn't been able to for several weeks. The lines slip away from her, become jumbled. She can't concentrate. She stays like that, with her eyes closed. She observes the relaxing of her limbs, waiting for the tension to lessen little by little.

But not today. She can't do it. Something is resisting, deep down, she can feel it, something which won't let go. A sort of anger that her body can't rid itself of, something within her which is in fact swelling.

'Don't you know it? It's a really well-known cream in the tanning world.'

The man burst out laughing. Mathilde opened her eyes. Several faces had turned towards him. Sitting on the seat opposite, the girl shook her head, no, she didn't know this cream, however incredible that might seem. They both had the same tanned complexion, verging on orange. Mathilde concluded that they must work in a tanning salon.

There are such things. These people work in the tanning world. Others in the nightlife or the restaurant world, or in the fashion world or television. Or even in conditioner.

In what world do undertakers work?

And what world does she belong to? The world of cowards, the weak, the quitters?

In the tunnel before the gare de Lyon, the train stopped. The lights went out, then the noise of the engine ceased. Silence descended suddenly. Mathilde looks around, her eyes struggle to adjust. No one is speaking any more, even Mr Orange has gone quiet.

People seem on guard, in the darkness their pupils shine.

She's stuck in the middle of a tunnel, shut in the lower part of a double-decker carriage, she's breathing damp air, saturated with carbon monoxide. It's too dark for her to make out the expressions of confidence on other people's faces which might reassure her. Conversations are slow to pick up again.

Suddenly it seems to her as though they are linked in a drama that is about to happen. They have been picked by fate, it's their turn this time. Something serious is going to happen.

She's never been afraid in the RER, even late at night, even when she goes home after 9 p.m., when the trains are almost empty. But today there's something in the air that constricts her chest, or else she's the one who's not OK, who's out of her depth.

She's in danger, she can feel it, an immense danger, though she cannot tell if it's inside or outside her, a danger which takes her breath away.

Ten minutes later an announcement informs passengers that the train has stopped in the middle of the track. In case they haven't noticed.

The conductor requests that they don't attempt to open the doors.

The lights come back on.

The man from the tanning salon starts speaking again. A wave of relief ripples out around him.

At last the train moves again and is greeted with a general 'ah'.

Mathilde gets off at the gare de Lyon. She retraces her route from this morning in the opposite direction.

At the interchange she tries to hurry, to fit herself into the flow.

She can't. It's going too fast.

Underground, the traffic rules are inspired by the highway code. You overtake on the left, and slow vehicles are requested to keep to the right.

Underground, there are two categories of traveller. The first follow their line as though they are suspended above the void, their path obeys precise rules from which they never deviate. By virtue of a wise desire to save time and effort, their movements are accurate to the nearest yard. You can tell them by the speed they walk at, the way they take the corners, and the impossibility of catching their eye. The other category dawdles, stops dead, they allow themselves to be carried along and go off at tangents without warning. The haphazardness of their path threatens the whole system. They interrupt the flow, throw the crowd off balance. They are the tourists, the disabled, the weak. If they don't keep themselves to one side, the herd takes on the task of excluding them.

So Mathilde stays on the right, sticks to the wall. She withdraws so as not to get in the way.

On the stairs she holds on to the handrail.

Suddenly she again wants to scream. Scream till her throat hurts, scream to block out the noise of footsteps and conversations. Scream so loud that everyone falls silent, everything is interrupted, stops moving. She would like to scream: 'Get out of here! Look what you have become! Look what we have become! Look at your dirty hands and pale faces. Look at what filthy insects we are, crawling beneath the earth, repeating the same actions day after day under the neon lights. Your body wasn't made for this. Your body should be able to move freely.'

Mathilde goes through the doors that mark the entrance to the metro.

At the point where several lines meet, there's anarchy. In the absence of markings on the floor, you have to cut across the current, create your own route.

There are those who get out of the way to avoid a collision of bodies, and those who consider by virtue of some vague right that other people should get out of their way.

This evening Mathilde goes towards the platform, looking straight ahead, as though she's been struck full force.

This evening she feels like the entire surface of her skin has become permeable. She is a mobile antenna linked to the aggression around her, a flexible antenna, bent in two.

If he looked at his watch, he'd know how long he's been there, trapped in his car, stuck behind a 4×4 with smoked-glass windows. If he looked at his watch, he would start crying.

It's jammed, blocked, paralysed. In front, behind, everywhere.

All around him.

From time to time, a cacophony of horns starts up, drowning out the sound of his CD player.

For as far as he can see, the traffic is stationary. Shops are beginning to pull down their shutters, lights are starting to come on in some buildings. Furtive shapes at windows are assessing the extent of the damage.

The man in front has turned off his engine. He's got out of his car and is smoking a cigarette.

Thibault rests his head on the steering wheel for a few seconds. He's never seen this before.

He could turn on the radio, listen to the news. He'd probably find out why things are so jammed.

He doesn't give a fuck.

The city has closed on him like a trap.

The man gets back in his car and moves forward a few yards. Thibault takes his foot off the brake and freewheels.

That's when he notices a parking place, *almost* a parking place on the right. A vacant space into which he should be able to manoeuvre himself.

He has to get out of this fucking car.

He'll leave it there and take the metro. He'll come back and get it tomorrow.

He makes several attempts, full lock in each direction, and ends up managing it, with one wheel up on the kerb. He picks up his case and his raincoat and slams the door.

He walks to the nearest station. At the foot of the stairs, he looks at the map, works out the shortest route home. He buys a ticket at the counter and takes the stairs to the platform.

He approaches the tracks and puts his case down.

He stands waiting.

Opposite him, the posters are full of summer light. Opposite him, the posters are showing off their sarongs, their golden beaches and their turquoise seas.

The city that crushes human beings is inviting them to relax.

O n the platform, Mathilde stopped in front of a vending machine. The electronic sign was announcing the next train in four minutes.

She thought that if she sat down she would never be able to get up again.

She looked at the women's bodies, their endless legs, smooth and tanned, the sun creams and the bottles of mineral water. And then the posters got jumbled, confused into a single moving canvas, a kaleidoscope of bright colours which spun around her. She felt her body pitching, she closed her eyes.

Later, as the platform filled up, a veil descended upon the whole station, a veil of dark tulle which reduced the intensity of the light.

The people were erased, she could feel their presence, sense their movements, but couldn't distinguish their faces any more.

Her legs were giving way beneath her, very gently. She was holding the Argent Defender card in her right hand; it seemed to her that she was leaning on him, that he was carrying her.

People were talking among themselves, braying into phones, listening to music which leaked from their headphones.

The noise from the people grew louder. The noise from the people grew unbearable.

Mathilde went closer to the track to look for the train. She leaned to the left, peering into the darkness of the tunnel. In the distance she thought she could make out the engine's headlights.

She stumbled against something, a bag or a case.

The man said: 'Shit, can't you look where you're going?'

When he bent down to pick up what looked like a doctor's bag, Mathilde noticed his left hand. It had only three fingers.

She passed in front of him. She felt the man's eyes watching her movements, she sensed his gaze on her back. She didn't have the courage to meet his eyes, or anything else around her, her whole body was taken up with remaining upright.

The train came into the station, the warm air it stirred up blew against her face. She closed her eyes for barely a second to avoid the dust.

She stepped back to wait for the doors to open and let people off.

She got into a carriage in the middle of the train, and slumped down on a folding seat. The train set off with a lurching motion, she felt sick.

The man with the case was now sitting in front of her, looking at her.

S ome outlines attract attention because they are longer or more fragile. The woman was blonde and wearing a big black coat. He noticed her at once. She was standing too close to the edge, unsteady, half stumbling, which the people around her didn't seem to notice. But he did. She came nearer to him and he almost told her to move away, she was standing so close.

The woman tripped over his case and moved away without apologising. He said 'shit' or 'fuck', or some equally choice expression. Words which were not his own. Tiredness was all it had taken to turn him into this hypersensitive creature, whose violence had been bottled up for too long and might explode at any moment.

When the train arrived, Thibault sat opposite her so that he could keep watching her. Why he found this woman so fascinating he couldn't have said. Nor why he wanted to talk to her.

*

The woman was avoiding his eye. It seemed to him that she was getting paler and paler. She sat up straighter to hold on to the rail. About ten passengers got on at the next station, and she had to give up her folding seat. He kept looking at her and then he told himself he couldn't keep staring at a woman like that.

He took his mobile out of his pocket and checked yet again that he didn't have a message.

He kept his gaze lowered for a few minutes. He thought about his apartment, about the warmth of the alcohol which would soon course through his veins, about the bath he would run later in the evening. He thought that he could no longer go backwards. He had left Lila. He had done it.

And then again he looked for the woman, beyond the mass of bodies – her feverish eyes, her blonde hair. This time she met his eye. After a few seconds it seemed to him that the woman's face was changing imperceptibly, even if nothing had actually shifted, nothing at all, that it was registering a sort of surprise or abandon. He couldn't have said which.

It seemed to him that he and this woman shared the same kind of exhaustion, a dispossession of the self which cast the body towards the ground. It seemed to him that he and this woman had lots of things in common. That was absurd and childish. He looked down again.

When the doors opened again, most of the passengers got out. He looked for her in the tightly packed crowd.

The train moved off. The woman had disappeared.

He closed his eyes for a few minutes.

The train slowed again and Thibault stood up. There was something shining on the floor. He picked up a role-play card with a strange name and held it in his hand for a few seconds.

The doors opened and he got off. He threw the card in the first bin he came to, then took the stairs that led to the corridor to another line.

Carried along by the dense, disorganised tide, he thought that the city would always impose its own rhythms, its haste, its rush hours, that it would always remain unaware of these millions of solitary journeys at whose points of intersection there is nothing. Nothing but a void, or else a spark that instantly goes out.

A NOTE ON THE AUTHOR

Delphine de Vigan is the author of *No and Me*, which was a bestseller in France and was awarded the Prix des Libraires (The Booksellers' Prize) in 2008. Her other novels include *Jolis garçons* and *Soir de décembre*. *Underground Time* was shortlisted for the 2009 Prix Goncourt.

A NOTE ON THE TRANSLATOR

George Miller is the translator of *No and* Me. He is also a regular translator for *Le Monde diplomatique*'s English-language edition, and the translator of *Conversations with my Gardener* by Henri Cueco and *Inside Al-Qaeda* by Mohammed Sifaoui.

A NOTE ON THE TYPE

The text of this book is set in Baskerville, and is named after
John Baskerville of Birmingham (1706–1775). The original
punches cut by him still survive. His widow sold them to
Beaumarchais, from where they passed through several
French foundries to Deberney & Peignot in Paris, before
finding their way to Cambridge University Press.

Baskerville was the first of the 'transitional romans'
between the softer and rounder calligraphic Old Face and
the 'Modern' sharp-tooled Bodoni. It does not look very
different to the Old Faces, but the thick and thin strokes are
more crisply defined, and the serifs on lower-case letters are
closer to the horizontal with the stress nearer the vertical.
The R in some sizes has the eighteenth-century curled tail,
the lower-case w has no middle serif, and the lower-case g
has an open tail and a curled ear.